Dear Romance Reader,

Welcome to a world of breathtaking passion and never-ending romance.
Welcome to *Precious Gem Romances.*

It is our pleasure to present *Precious Gem Romances,* a wonderful new line of romance books by some of America's best-loved authors. Let these thrilling historical and contemporary romances sweep you away to far-off times and places in stories that will dazzle your senses and melt your heart.

Sparkling with joy, laughter, and love, each *Precious Gem Romance* glows with all the passion and excitement you expect from the very best in romance. Offered at a great affordable price, these books are an irresistible value—and an essential addition to your romance collection. Tender love stories you will want to read again and again, *Precious Gem Romances* are books you will treasure forever.

Look for eight fabulous new *Precious Gem Romances* each month—available only at Wal★Mart.

Lynn Brown, Publisher

# DESIRE'S DISGUISE

## Kathryn Kramer

**ZEBRA BOOKS**
**KENSINGTON PUBLISHING CORP.**

*To Paul Ehrmann, screenwriter, actor and treasured friend, who shares my love of theater, adventure, sunsets and mountains. This story is for you with love. . . .*

ZEBRA BOOKS are published by

Kensington Publishing Corp.
850 Third Avenue
New York, NY 10022

First Printing: August, 1996
10 9 8 7 6 5 4 3 2 1

Printed in the United States of America

# Author's Note

Theatrical performances were forbidden in England from 1642 until 1660, during the rule of the Commonwealth and the Protectorate of Oliver Cromwell. The Globe Theater, made famous during the days of Shakespeare, was torn down. Performers were forced to go underground, and Parliament passed a new law ordering that all actors be apprehended as rogues.

Upon the restoration of the monarchy theaters were quickly revived, however. Londoners clamored for entertainment, and rival theatrical companies sprang up, including a number of troupes that performed in the provinces. This renewed interest in plays created a problem, namely, the acquisition of a suitable repertory.

Shakespeare's dramas were revived and revised to bring them up to date. *Romeo and Juliet, Macbeth, Hamlet,* and other works were given a second reign of popularity. Older plays that were too outmoded were dropped as soon as new ones were available. Though playwrights were discovered, none of their works are very popular today.

New theaters were erected, including the Theater Royal on Bridges Street and the Drury Lane. In 1661 Lisle's Tennis Court was converted into the Lincoln's Inn Fields Theater.

During Shakespeare's day men took on women's roles, but a major innovation of the Restoration was the inclusion of women in acting companies. Men appeared now only in such female roles as witches and comic old women. By 1661 acting companies had a full complement of actresses.

A whole new world had been opened to women, that of the stage. The incomes of performers varied considerably, but it was possible for an actor or actress to make a quite comfortable living and even to own shares in the acting company.

Performances were advertised by posters set up around the city and by handbills distributed at coffee houses and to private homes. Thus was added a new dimension to performing, fame. While the theater was becoming firmly established, this was also the age of highwaymen, liaisons, intrigue, and religious strife. It was an interesting time.

A young woman faced a turbulent and changing world, therefore, when she was forced to flee her country home. Taking upon herself a whole new persona, she would undoubtedly find adventure . . . and love.

# Part One:
# The Visitor
## England—1664

"Love sought is good, but given unsought is better."

—Shakespeare, *Twelfth Night*

# One

The three-storied, thatched-roof houses of Reedham leaned toward each other like gossiping neighbors. Far to the north, at the edge of the houses stood the Rose and Thorn inn, a half-timbered whitewashed building, distinctive with its bright red shutters and large wooden sign that beckoned visitors. Kimberly pushed at those shutters, viewing the bright spring day from the open window.

"Beautiful. . . !"

Red, blue, yellow, pink, and white flowers added brilliant color to the once dormant garden and gave off an enchanting perfume. For just a moment as her eyes scanned the beautiful blooms, life at her uncle's shabby old tavern did not seem quite so dismal. As long as she still had her dreams, she was afforded some escape from the drudgery.

"At least Uncle Harold can't take this away from me. . . ."

Kimberly had lived with her uncle, Harry Bowen, since the death of her mother a year and a half ago. Left penniless and homeless, she had sought out her mother's brother, thankful to have someone she could call "family." He had shown her little sympathy, however, quickly putting her to work for her board and lodging and thus allowing her little time to mourn.

"Busy is as busy does" was her uncle's favorite saying. Certainly it had proven to be true. It seemed that Kimberly was ever busy. There was always some chore to do. Recently she had been given the added task of serving in the inn's taproom, a duty she detested because of the pawing hands, the bawdy suggestive remarks and the bold stares of the customers. Worse yet, Kimberly knew she was being used as bait to lure some of the paunchy gentry to the tavern. So much for her uncle's "hospitality."

She stared into the diamond panes of the mullioned window. She had been told by the inn's patrons that she had a flawless complexion, high cheekbones, large blue eyes and teeth that were perfectly straight. Ha! Little good such blessings did her. Her face and the gentle swell of her bosom were her mother's only legacy. That and hard work. The good woman had toiled at housework and as a seamstress to keep food on the table and a roof over their heads. Even when she had been stricken with illness, she had pushed herself beyond endurance, finally leaving her daughter all alone in the world. Now that she was gone, Kimberly could only pray she had at last found peace.

"And someday. . . ." It was Kimberly's dream to have a home of her own—anywhere at all—a place she could do just as she pleased without having to ask permission.

Her moments away from the tavern were unfortunately few. Even so, whenever she had a few extra coins and a minute to herself, she would go to the theater. While attending the performances, she would stare intently at the beautiful women who walked so gracefully around the stage, and for just a little while all her troubles were forgotten as she gave herself up to the fantasy.

Kimberly leaned on the handle of her mop, enjoying the fresh early morning air. She loved mornings. They were peaceful. Quiet. Her uncle's scolding voice was silenced by sleep. He would be abed at least until noon, and though she was expected to clean the inn from top to bottom; make all the beds; wash mugs, cups, tankards and plates; do all the sweeping, mopping and dusting, she was able to enjoy her solitude.

A soft breeze, filled with the sharp scent of the Thames, stirred the foliage on the trees. Kimberly let the soft wind caress her face and stir her blond hair for a long moment. Tomorrow was her birthday. That thought caused her to stiffen.

Twenty. It sounded so old. The time had gone much too quickly. It seemed she was working her life away. Oh, how she wanted to be free.

"I want to be far, far away from here," she whispered.

With that thought in mind she had been very frugal with the coins the patrons sometimes gave her. Except for her occasional attendance at the theater, she carefully saved each and every penny, stashing the coins beneath her mattress in a small leather purse. That money was the only chance she had for freedom.

*Freedom!*

"I cannot spend another winter beneath this roof." She had her pride and resented the surly treatment she received from her uncle. It seemed, no matter how hard she worked or how much she tried to please him, Harold never smiled or showed her any kindness. Even worse was the way he talked about her mother, insisting that she had brought about her own self-destruction. Harold Bowen never ceased to jabber on about how he had warned his sister not to fall in love with any faithless soldiers.

"She wouldn't listen, and you can see where her stubbornness led her," he would say. He insisted that Kimberly could be just as stubborn. Well, perhaps she could be on occasion.

With a sigh of resignation, Kimberly went indoors, wrinkling up her nose in disgust as she stepped inside. The taproom smelled of smoke, grease, stale wine and beer. Although she would mop the floor and clean the walls from floorboards to ceiling it would smell the same tomorrow morning.

Kimberly filled a bucket with water and soap. As she worked her mind soared beyond her drab surroundings. Her dress was not made out of dull brown cotton but of lace and velvet. Her long golden hair wasn't drawn back in a bun, but was piled high atop her head. Diamonds studded her ears and the necklace at her throat. Surrendering to the dream, she glided across the floor, her shoulders thrust back and her chin pointed up at just the right angle.

" 'A rose by any other name . . .' " she declaimed. Ah, that was how she would think of herself. A wild rose, and she would—

A voice startled her. "B'God, if you aren't a rare beauty!"

Kimberly whirled around. "Who . . . ?" Her face flushed with embarrassment. She had thought herself to be all alone in the room. Now she felt foolish as a tall, handsome man sauntered up. "The taproom is not open!" she informed him.

"That's quite all right. It's far too early to drink." He stood there, just staring at her; then he smiled. "I think perhaps I would as sooth just look at you."

"At me?" Self-consciously she ran her fingers through her hair, then brushed at her apron, moving away from the glare of the sunlight streaming through the mullioned windows. Out of the corners of her eyes she assessed the stranger. He wasn't at all like the usual sort who came here. He didn't have the paunchy belly caused from too much drink, nor did he have the ever-flushed face of those prone to ale. This man was tall and muscular, with a bold look about him despite his blue velvet suit. Wisps of dark tousled hair fell into his eyes and brushed against his collar.

For a moment it was a duel of stares. His eyes swept over her again, appraisingly, lingering on the rise and fall of her breasts, then touching on her face. "Pretty. Very, very pretty." She was wide-eyed. Innocently fair. Her long hair was drawn back from her face, a few tendrils curling about her temples, yet there was a sensuality to her full mouth and long-lashed eyes.

"Have you ever wanted to be an actress?" he inquired.

"Actress? Me?" Kimberly smoothed the wrinkles from her skirt.

"Aye. You!" There was a smudge of dirt on her nose which he gently removed with the tip of his finger.

Kimberly's hair was coming undone from the confines of her hairpins, the skirt beneath her apron was threadbare and badly in need of mending. His scrutiny suddenly made her aware of all such flaws.

"Don't worry. Even dressed in a miller's sack you would be lovely." Green eyes looked back at her. There was a self-assurance in them, as if he were a man who knew his self-worth.

"Thank . . . thank you."

He grinned. "How I envy your husband."

Kimberly's face burned as she realized what he meant. "I'm not married."

"You are an untried maiden, then?" His eyebrows quirked, asking a silent question. Was she, his look seemed to say? "Perhaps you need a protector?"

"Certainly not." She quickly lowered her eyes from his piercing gaze. "I have food and shelter aplenty."

"And are you paid a good wage?"

"I live here and work for my uncle. He owns the tavern," she replied, hoping her tone didn't sound too forlorn.

He could well imagine, having seen *that* man, how exciting her life must be. From his point of view her uncle looked much like an ogre, and was far too grumpy and unpleasant to be good company for this young woman. She needed to be around someone who would make her feel alive, vibrant. He could see loneliness written all over her face.

Always one to speak his mind, he came right to the point. "A woman as lovely as you should never be without lovemaking."

His bold manner shocked her. "Sir!"

He had the effrontery to laugh at her stunned reaction, then said more somberly, "If you are of a mind for passion and tender words of love, I'll tell you without the threat of boasting that I'm your man." He'd bring a smile to those grimly tensed lips.

"I have need for . . . for love," she said with a toss of her head. "I have work to do!" Kimberly turned her back on him in much the same manner she used with other overbold men. She knew what he was going to say next. She'd heard it all before, too many times to count. It seemed that just because a man's thoughts were always in his breeches, he expected women to be the same. Well, she was a decent girl and would allow no man, no matter how handsome, to say such things to her.

He eyed her hopefully, then shrugged his shoulders. "Just an observation and an invitation if you find yourself with a longing."

Kimberly was incensed by his behavior. A "longing" he called it. "If I had such . . . such feelings I wouldn't give in to . . . to sin. It's a wedding ring I'll wait for."

Again he laughed. "Aha! A spirited wench." When she made it a point to ignore him he took a step closer and said in her ear, "I like a woman who puts a high price on her virtue. . . ."

A quiver danced up and down her spine as she felt his breath tickle her ear. Her heart was pounding so loudly she was certain he could hear.

"It makes the chase all the more thrilling."

"The chase . . . ?" With a gasp she started to pull away, but his hand tightened on her shoulder, halting her departure.

His voice quieted to a rumbling, seductive whisper. "Don't be afraid. I mean you no harm. I was merely telling the truth. A woman like you should be cherished, held against a man's heart. Comforted. Loved." His tone was a low rasp that touched every nerve in her body. "Never lonely."

He had touched upon her vulnerability. She *was* lonely. Terribly so. It was true, she did long for a man's arms around her. There were times when she craved kisses and caresses. Nevertheless she answered tartly, "I am not lonely!"

He turned her around to face him. "Perhaps not. . . ."

She found herself close to him, so close that her breasts lightly brushed against his hard chest. Close enough that one flyaway lock of her hair tickled his stubbled cheek and then slid free.

"Men undoubtedly hover around you like bees to a rose."

"Yes. . . . No!" She thought of her uncle's leering patrons and grimaced.

"Ah, so that is it. The kind of men you meet here are hardly the kind to inspire a young woman's dreams. Such a pity."

She was all too aware of the rippling muscles in his thighs as his legs moved against hers, but though she could very well have pushed him away, she didn't do so. The contact of their bodies was much too pleasant. She looked at the chiseled strength of his lips and found herself wondering how his mouth would feel upon her own. Oh, how different he was from the others.

He looked deep into her eyes, sensing her attraction to him. Tipping her chin up with one lean finger he kissed her mouth before she could sense his intentions. It was a surprisingly gentle kiss for all his strength, and though she tried to ignore the flicker of warmth that spread from her mouth to the core of her body, she could not. It was an enjoyable sensation, a pleasurable tingle.

Kimberly closed her eyes, pressing close to him. Her lips trembled beneath the heated encroachment of his. This man knew exactly what he was doing. Clinging to him, she relished his strength, letting his lips and tongue explore hers. She could feel his heart pounding against her breasts as his kiss deepened. How long he kissed her she didn't know. All she could think about was the singing in her heart as his mouth devoured hers.

"Mmmm."

His arms went around her waist, pulling her even tighter against him. "Your mouth is every bit as soft as it looked to be," he said at last when he lifted his lips from hers.

She lifted her eyes to meet his gaze, knowing that if he hadn't been holding her she would have fallen. Her heart was beating so hard it seemed to shake her whole body. She couldn't think, couldn't breathe. What was happening to her? Kissing this handsome stranger was very pleasant, and yet there was something else. Something that she sensed could be dangerous. With that thought in mind she found the willpower to pull away.

"Oh, no, sweetling. Don't draw away!" He kept her imprisoned in a tender embrace. He'd soon take her mind off toiling in this godforsaken tavern. She needed him, even if she didn't realize it. "Life is all too short. Come, let's not waste one precious moment of the morning."

"Sir!"

He ignored her protest. With a self-assured grin, he positioned one arm behind her knees, the other at her hips, to sweep her up into his arms.

"Sir!" Kimberly said again, struggling against him, pulling away. She was outraged by his assumption that she could be bedded so easily. Even her uncle's most daring customers had never been so impudent. "Leave me be!" Though she meant what she said, he seemed amused by her angry outburst, as if he didn't take her refusal seriously. Soft laughter met her protests as he swept her into his arms.

"Don't tell me no. There's no sense in playing it coy." He was tiring of her game of protestation when he knew she felt otherwise. Boldly he headed toward the stairs.

"No!" In a panic, Kimberly struggled to get free. "No!" she said again. "I have work to do, and—"

Playfully he nuzzled her ear. "So do I, however it would be much more pleasurable to dally first." He tugged insistently at her hand.

"Oh!" He just wouldn't listen, and Kimberly's temper flared. Still, she was horrified by what happened next, for without really reflecting on her actions she had picked up a mug of ale and tossed it in his face. Then she was running from the taproom as fast as her legs could carry her and not once looking back.

# Two

The tavern smelled of stale ale, but also of grease and smoke from the nearby kitchen's stove. These odors assailed Christopher Sheldon's nostrils as he sat with his feet propped up on the table. Despite them, he was hungry. He hadn't eaten breakfast and was impatient for the noon hour. The rumble in his stomach only added to his surly mood.

"She could have said no in a more delicate way," he rasped, remembering his surprise when she had flung the contents of the mug at him. And yet he couldn't really blame her. She was defending her virtue from his obvious intent. Still, he wished their encounter had ended differently.

That kiss had teased him with the promise of what could have been. Her soft, yielding mouth had tasted sweet and had unleashed his desires the moment his mouth had touched hers. He had sensed the smoldering embers within her just waiting to be ignited into passion by the right man. B'God, he was the one. Why then had she so urgently doused the flame? She had fled up the stairs like a frightened mouse, hiding herself away. He on the other hand, had hung around the taproom all morning in the hope of catching sight of her. He, Christopher Sheldon, London's greatest actor was smitten, why not admit it? Ah yes, she was a challenge, a temptation. Didn't he always seek such excitement and enticement?

Christopher's life had been filled with adventure, since as a headstrong young lad he'd ridden with the highwayman who was to become known as Gentleman James. Having fought for the restoration of Charles II to the English throne, he had taken his monetary reward and invested it in a theatrical company, of which he was the main attraction. Women were at his beck and call. It had been a life of varied pleasures, vices and dangers. An adventurer was what he had become, though often he'd been called both rogue and scoundrel.

Recently returned from a tour with his theater company in France, Christopher was on his way to London to dazzle the city with a new play. One he had written himself. If the drama came perilously close to revealing the details of his own life, then so be it. As to the young woman, he meant to have her, to taste of her charms before he left the inn.

"B'God, if she thinks all it takes to cool my ardor is a slosh of ale she had better think again." Christopher always got what he wanted, and want her he did, even more so as he saw her walking slowly down the stairs.

Kimberly looked this way and that before entering the taproom. Indeed, she would have stayed above much longer if she had not heard her uncle rustling about in his room. If she neglected her duties this morning there would be trouble. Even her disquiet about another encounter with that dark-haired scoundrel wasn't worth such a to-do. Besides, by now that rogue would certainly be gone, she decided.

"Good morrow!"

The husky male voice startled her. Merry-go-up, it was him!

"I feared that you had disappeared." Christopher's generous mouth curved in a smile as he stood up and made a polite bow.

"You!"

"Aye. Me." He cleared his throat, then said, "Allow me to introduce myself. Mister Christopher Sheldon. Just plain Chris I prefer to be called."

Kimberly stiffened, eyeing him warily. *"Mister* Sheldon," she said icily, refusing to allow him to be familiar. The name sounded vaguely familiar as it tripped from her lips. Sheldon.

Even so, her only thought was to remove herself quickly from his company lest there be another scene. She moved briskly toward the door with that thought in mind, but Christopher Sheldon, with the grace of a cat, blocked her exit.

"Nay, don't go."

"Pray tell. I must be about my chores," she answered with a toss of her head.

"I know, I know. But please, hear me out for just a moment."

She shrugged. "All right."

"I frightened you this morning, unknowingly and unthinkingly insulted your . . . uh . . . virtue. I just want to say I'm sorry." Though his mouth held its usual smile, he sounded sincere.

"You're apologizing."

"I am." He held out his hand, as a man usually did to another. "Can I make amends?"

He really was very personable. How could she hold a grudge? Besides, the more she lingered in his presence the more Kimberly liked this Christopher. "All right. I'll accept your apology, if you promise to mind your manners."

"I promise to be as circumspect as the King," he answered, mocking that royal womanizer. His teeth were a glowing white that contrasted sharply with the bronze of his face and the darkness of his hair. "You have my word."

"Circumspect, indeed." By his tone he was making light of their encounter, angering her anew. She did not like his teasing manner.

"I will. . . ."

Regrettably Christopher had little self-control when it came to women. Despite his promise he was all too tempted by her well-shaped bottom as she sauntered past him. Impulsively he reached out to give it a gentle whack.

"Uhhhhhh!" Kimberly gasped. Moving toward the fire she grabbed up a large fork and wielded it like a weapon.

"Truce!" He waved his hands in the air.

Forsooth he unnerved her, confused her with contradicting emotions. Her instincts warned that he was dangerous. Even so, she put down the fork. It would not do to cause a stir in the inn by wounding him. Besides, if one were to ostracize every rogue and scoundrel in the town there'd scarce be anyone left to talk to.

"We'll make peace, but just for the moment."

With an exaggerated motion, he took her hand. " 'Tis a start."

The caress of his fingers stirred something deep within her. Struggling to appear poised, she betrayed herself as she lowered her eyes from his gaze. "I'm not . . . not that kind of woman . . . I . . . I—"

"I know." He stroked the palm of her hand with his fingers, pausing as he felt the calluses and blisters.

"I work very hard for my uncle, keeping the inn clean and working in the taproom."

He saw the evidence for himself and damned the man under his breath. "Your uncle must have no compassion to condemn such a lovely young woman to working her life away. Were you mine, I would pamper you instead." Lifting her hand to his face, he pressed his warm mouth into her soft flesh in a gesture he had learned from Gentleman James himself. It had always worked to charm a lady.

Kimberly's heart took flight. "Were I yours?"

His voice was like a caress. "Aye, were you mine I would give you the world." He raised his brows, inquiring silently about her name.

"Kimberly. 'Tis Kimberly."

"Kimberly! It suits you."

"My mother gave me the name." She couldn't help but be curious about him, but she didn't want to ask prying questions.

"Your mother?"

"She died two years ago of a fever"

"Oh! I'm sorry." He was, knowing how gut-wrenchingly

sad it was to lose one's mother. "Is your uncle, then, your only family?"

"He is." Kimberly's brows drew together in a frown, an expression Christopher couldn't help but notice. "He took me in when my mother died because I had no place else to go." She had too much pride to tell him any more.

"How *kind* of him." He couldn't keep the sarcasm from his voice. No doubt that long-nosed innkeeper uncle of hers made her work her fingers to the bone. He looked the type.

"In reality I suppose it was. He could have turned me away." A harsh truth. "But what of you?"

"I have no one." Seeing sympathy clearly written in her eyes, he amended, "At least I hadn't until Tobias and James took me in."

"James?"

Oh, how he loved to tell the story. "Have you heard the tales about Gentleman James?"

"The highwayman?"

The excitement in her voice caused him to laugh softly. "Aye, the highwayman. When I was but a lad I traveled the roads with him. And nearly got hung in the bargain." Relishing an avid listener, he began the story of what had happened to him in those exciting days upon the heath. "It was dangerous, mysterious. . . ."

Kimberly listened intently, wanting to know as much about him as she could. He was certainly the most interesting man she'd ever come in contact with. "And . . . and are you still?"

Throwing back his head, he laughed. "Oh, no! All the sword-fighting I do now is on the stage. As I said, I'm an actor." That was nearly as interesting as being a highwayman. "London's very best."

Christopher Sheldon, she thought, the name running over and over in her mind. Now she knew why she recognized it. She'd seen him in a play several months ago. He was not the kind of man a woman would forget.

"You played Romeo. . . ."

"A part I'm definitely suited for . . ." He might have said more, had not the young woman's uncle come upon the scene.

"I have to go!" Kimberly looked anxiously in the direction of Harold Bowen. She didn't want him to embarrass her in front of this man with a tongue-lashing. Lifting up the hem of her skirt she moved toward her uncle, but paused to look over her shoulder at Christopher just long enough to bask in the warmth of his smile. She wouldn't have admitted to herself for the world how his grin affected her. Most certainly not. But it did. Nonetheless, lifting her chin, she walked with dignified grace across the room.

Kimberly knew that Christopher's eyes followed her. She tried to tell herself the newcomer's attentions were unwanted, but knew that to be a lie. His presence was stimulating and put a tinge of excitement in her ordinarily routine day. Certainly he was a fascinating man, one who brought to mind the excitement and glamor of the stage. Handsome. Bold. Daring. *What if I could convince him to take me with him?*

"Kimberly! Move about, girl. You are taking much too long with your chores."

"Yes, of course. You are right." Kimberly didn't want to argue with him, especially not with Christopher Sheldon in the room. Snatching up a broom, she wielded it with a fury, purposefully putting as great a distance between them as she could, throwing all her attention into the task.

Christopher Sheldon watched the pretty golden-haired woman work, and he could not help but feel a twinge of admiration. That odious ogre of an uncle made her toil endlessly, yet she never uttered one word of complaint. It seemed the one thing Kimberly had plenty of was patience. He smiled, however, at her audible sigh when at last her uncle tired of watching her and left the room. For the moment at least she had some respite from the man's unpleasantries.

If it was the last thing he did before he left here, he'd see a smile turn up the corners of that soft, rosebud mouth. From what he could see of her life here, she needed more than a lover, however. She needed a guardian angel. Him? Perhaps.

Christopher watched her for a long moment. Just what kind of a woman was she? There was something vulnerable about her. It made her all the more alluring somehow. Even so, her movements had a certain unaffected sensuality. She was an interesting combination of siren and saint.

Though he seldom put himself out unless for a profit, Christopher found himself hefting up a heavy pail. He carried it across the room. "Allow me."

"Thank you," she said appreciatively, looking at him from the corners of her eyes. She was going to tell him that she didn't need his help, but the words just didn't come. Maybe because she really *did* and had been hoping he'd come to her rescue.

Their fingers brushed for just an instant as she reached for the handle of the bucket to regain her burden. The magic of his masculine, commanding presence was making it harder and harder to keep her resolve. Although she knew she should have been shunning his companionship, she now found herself welcoming it. She suspected it would be all too easy to fall in love with him. He was bold and exciting, more than just a little mesmerizing. She was already feeling the pull of his charm in that most secret place in her heart. She would have to be wary, or so she told herself over and over again.

Throughout the rest of the day, into late afternoon Christopher gave her aid, carrying buckets, emptying out the dirty water and filling them with clean. He even located another broom and moved it briskly over the wooden floor. He told himself that his sudden act of gallantry was due to his tarrying with her this morning and thus was partly responsible for her tasks not getting done promptly, but that was an untruth. Damned if it wasn't just because he liked her company and would seek it even if that meant helping her in her work. He told her stories about his travels as they spent the time side by side, basking in the warmth of laughter.

"A smile becomes you," he whispered. "You should smile more often."

"I will now that you have come along. . . ." She blushed, realizing what she had said. *Now that he had come along.* Certainly he'd transformed the day into something special. But tomorrow or the next day or the one after, he would leave and she would never see him again. Unless . . .

Once again the thought of going with him tugged at her brain, but she quickly rejected it. No, if she was going to escape her uncle's domineering presence it would have to be on her own.

# Three

From the planked floor to the low-beamed ceiling the taproom was bathed in firelight and candle glow. Flames in the large hearth danced about, spewing tongues of red and orange that illuminated the faces of the men seated around the tavern's tables. The taproom was thronged with patrons who filled the air with their boisterous laughter and mumbled voices. The laughter and chatter was deafening, so much so that Kimberly could barely concentrate. It was just the kind of evening she detested, for she knew what was to follow. The assemblage of louts would grope, fondle and stare, and she would not be allowed to defend herself.

"I want you to keep them happy, for to do so is to keep them here," her uncle would insist. Scurrying from table to table and back to the door, he personally greeting his most favored customers. "Kimberly, don't just stand there, silly wench. Bring our special wine."

Filling several glasses with the pungent-smelling red liquid, Kimberly balanced them on a tray. She glanced apprehensively toward a table of thirsty, rowdy men as she passed them, and somehow managing to dodge their pinches and pats to come unmolested to her uncle's side.

"Your wine . . . !" One particularly loathsome man of wealth was watching her with more than the usual intent, so much so that one might have thought he'd never seen her before. It made her shiver. Undoubtedly the man was going to be troublesome tonight, she sensed it. She could not count on her uncle, however, to guard her virtue.

Christopher was another matter entirely. Keeping his eyes riveted on her, he watched protectively. They are all smitten by her, he thought, noting the way all eyes turned her way. And why not? She was beautiful, even in the drab garments of white and brown her uncle had her wear. His eyes swept over her, taking in the breasts that strained against the tight bodice. Her waist was small. He could span it with his hands. Her hips were just well rounded enough to be interesting.

And there was more to the young woman than being pertly pretty. Christopher was soon to find out that she could take care of herself. Adroitly dodging the questing pinches and pats with a skill that was admirable, she didn't lose her poise. Not once!

"Ah, my lady," he said aloud as she passed by his table, " 'Tis a wonder you be." He reached out and touched her hand just as her uncle cried out her name for the hundredth time that night.

"Kimberly! More wine, girl!"

When she started to move away, Christopher held her back. "Come, let the old goat pour the wine himself. Sit beside me if only for a few minutes."

"I can not!" She wanted to, for even his brief touch had stirred her heart, but she also wanted to avoid trouble, not for herself but for him. Harry Bowen could be a nasty lout if he were provoked.

Harry Bowen called out again.

"Kimberly, Kimberly, Kimberly," Christopher mocked, looking in the man's direction with unbridled anger. "Forsooth, I do not know how you refrain from killing the bastard," he muttered under his breath. "I think were I in your situation I would be tempted." He rose from his chair, of a mind to tell the old goat a thing or two.

Kimberly held him back. "No!" Christopher was outnumbered by the miscreants her uncle called "friends." She didn't want to see the handsome actor thrown out into the night for if that happened she might not see him again. "I must go. I have much to do!" She cast him a woeful smile.

Cups, mugs and glasses were filled and refilled. Throughout the evening as she carried her trays and mugs back and forth Kimberly could feel all the eyes upon her. Tonight, however, she didn't care. Not as long as *he* was there too.

"You foolish girl," she scolded herself. "Do you really think he cares?" Christopher Sheldon had his own life to live without giving a second thought to some tavern maid. Soon he would be gone, just like all the others, from her life. The only person she could count on was herself.

As usual the taproom's patrons kept her amply busy. Wine glasses, ale tankards, whiskey mugs were refilled over and over again, until finally the flames engulfing the huge logs in the hearth sputtered and burned low. Patrons who had warbled lewd songs were now sprawled upon the benches or snored as they cradled their heads on their hands.

One by one the smoking candles and torches that had brightened the taproom flickered, hissed and died out. Darkness gathered quickly under the tavern's low-beamed ceiling, shadows hovered in the corners like evil spirits waiting to pounce.

At last! Kimberly could retreat to her haven upstairs. Or at least she thought she could. Instead, as she passed by her uncle he grabbed her arm. "I saw you."

"Saw me?"

Harold Bowen's eyes hardened into two heated coals as he glared at her. "Making cow eyes at that dark-haired stranger. Well, I will not have it. I will not have you ending up like my sister, with a baby in your belly."

"Unless it can in some way profit you," she retorted hotly. "Were there enough money in it for you, 'tis obvious you would care little for my virtue. Well, I'm not for sale."

She turned to leave, but he barred her way, then gripped her arm tightly. "I will not have you talk to me that way, girl. Not after I so kindly took you in."

"Took me in?" She shuddered as she reflected on his "charity."

"Aye. I kept you from begging out in the streets. You owe me much." Roughly he gave her arm a painful twist.

"Ouch!" Kimberly fought to get free. "Let me go!" she commanded, but he wouldn't release her so easily.

"Come to think of it, you're a real little beauty," he said in a low tone. "Perhaps I didn't make a bad bargain after all. Perhaps I should do as you say and—"

"Sell me?" She laughed scornfully.

Her laughter infuriated him, and bringing back his hand, he slapped her cheek. The sound echoed through the quiet room.

"B'God!"

Kimberly gasped as Christopher's voice sliced through the darkness. A welcome sound. She felt a rush of relief.

"Turn her loose." Christopher's gaze remained locked on Kimberly, even as he spoke to her tormentor.

"This is a family affair and none of your business," Harry Bowen retorted. He held firm to Kimberly's arm.

"When you strike a woman you make it *my* business," Christopher said. "Let her go or so help me . . ." There was barely suppressed fury in his tone. "I'll count to three. One . . . two. . . ."

As if sensing that this was no bluff, Kimberly's uncle loosened his hold, putting his hands at his sides. Instead of running away, however, he made a fatal mistake. One of his patron's swords was discarded haphazardly on the floor. He picked it up.

"No!" Kimberly was horrified.

Christopher echoed her protest. "No! I will not duel with you. Violence is no answer." He would not be goaded into drawing the sword he carried upon this man.

"Then I call you coward!" Harry Bowen was in his cups and determined to cause trouble.

Christopher flinched, but he did not move. It would be an ill-matched contest. Let this man rant, let him rage, he would not draw his own sword. "We have no quarrel. I will not fight! All I ask is that you treat your niece with common decency, for she is a lady."

"She is bastard born."

Christopher stiffened, hurting for Kimberly's humiliation. "No matter the circumstances of her birth, she is a lady."

"Argh!"

Foolishly Harry Bowen lunged. Only by the grace of God was Christopher able to duck out of the way in time. Even so, he was determined to keep to his word not to draw his sword. Using an old wooden stool he blocked the man's blows again and again. It was like a tragic dance, a grotesque pantomime of sword thrusts and parrying. Tankards were spilled, tables overturned, as even the most drunken onlookers hurried to get out of the way.

Kimberly cried out as her uncle drove Christopher up against a wall. The look in his eyes boded no mercy. "Uncle, please. I beg you. Don't kill him." Her frantic cry distracted Bowen just long enough for Christopher to pull free. In desperation he was now forced to defend himself as Harry lunged blindly.

The tavern was in a state of pandemonium, of total confusion, as the fighting continued. Then for a moment everything occurred as if in slow motion. Harry Bowen gasped and groaned, then grunted. Opening his eyes wide in surprise, he slumped to the floor.

"Is he dead? Is he . . . ?" Kimberly's voice was a breathless whisper.

Christopher didn't even pause to find out. One look at the angry faces in the crowd told him not to dally here. Without so much as a backward glance, he moved toward the door, making his escape.

# Four

In all her days Kimberly had never felt such cold, stark fear. "Uncle . . . ! Uncle!" He didn't answer, nor did he move. Not an eyelid, not a finger, not a muscle. He couldn't be dead. Kimberly drew back, trying to control a fit of sudden trembling. Dear God, Christopher had killed him.

"He's been murdered!" someone cried.

"Cold-bloodedly . . . !" Fingers pointed, eyes stared.

"No, it wasn't like that. You saw! My uncle lunged first. Christopher was only defending himself."

Alas, her words were wasted. These men had been Harry Bowen's friends, his drinking companions. They owed no loyalty to Christopher, nor indeed to her!

"Her lover killed ole Harry."

"Aye, all because of a woman."

"Indeed; she was most likely in on't."

"Guilty as sin!"

Clasping her hands together, Kimberly tried to think rationally. Her every instinct screamed that she had to get away. Quickly. With a cry of revulsion, she took to her heels, pushing through the door. Running toward the bushes, she fled the inn.

Fear goaded her to run and run until she was exhausted. A wave of sickness washed over her as she thought about the gruesome scene that had so quickly unfolded. Her uncle had picked up a sword and attacked another man. Was it her fault? No. Nor was it Christopher's. He had merely been defending her. It little mattered that there had been provocation, however, for now he was in danger of losing his life.

"I'm Christopher's witness. I know what happened." But would anyone really care about the reality of the matter? Harry Bowen was a respected citizen with at least a hundred friends and patrons. They would view the circumstances of the sword fight from a biased viewpoint. What chance had Christopher? He would be hunted down unmercifully.

"Oh, dear God!" What would happen to Christopher? What would happen to *her?* Kimberly suddenly felt chilled. She'd never been so alone, so desolate.

Emotions welled up inside her like water ready to burst through a dam. Tears, which she had been cautiously holding in check for so many months, now rolled down her cheeks. Fiercely she dashed them away, sobbing as she stumbled and fell headlong in a heap upon the grass. Huddled in a ball, miserable, she gave vent to her fear and grief until her tears were spent.

She felt numb. Tired. Even so her instinct for survival was stronger than she might have imagined. Slowly rising to her feet, she wandered aimlessly for a long while, her mind awhirl in broken dreams and memories. What was she going to do now? She didn't really know. Where could she go? There was no one who would take her in. Her uncle had been her only relative. By all intents and purposes she was alone and friendless.

Curses and the sounds of running feet were carried to Kimberly's ears by the wind. Undoubtedly the townspeople had already raised a fuss. Hysteria would possess the townsmen. In the heat of their anger they'd cry for Christopher's punishment. They might even hang him!

"No!"

Picking up her skirts, she ran as fast as her legs would carry her. She had to do something to save Christopher. He had fought for her; now she must do likewise for him.

"We'll find him. He won't get far," John Travers answered.

"All the roads leaving town are blocked, thanks to my warning."

"He won't get away. . . ."

The square courtyard of the inn was in total pandemonium. Holding torches aloft, several of the townsmen were pacing about the inn's yard. The night's events had drawn an angry crowd that flitted about, chattering and questioning. From the uproar it was obvious the townsmen would leave no stone unturned until they found their quarry.

Kimberly was angered at the thought. These men had seen her uncle pick up the sword. They had viewed with their own eyes what had happened. Why then were they carrying on so? For the sake of justice or for the sake of petty revenge?

Every doorway and gateway of the inn was blocked. Kimberly feared that all too soon Christopher would be discovered, for where could he hide? Where could he be safe from detection? The question plagued her.

The moon, risen high, was teasing the inn yard with faint pulsating light. A huge chestnut tree stood sentinel, its limbs spread out like arms. Kimberly looked around, but the inn's grounds were deserted. There was no sign of Christopher. Thank God! Perhaps he had gotten away.

"Oh, Christopher!" Her voice was a silent croak against the night air as the night breeze stung her eyes, blending with her tears. "Christopher!"

"Psssssst."

The sound wasn't any louder than the buzz of a bee, yet Kimberly heard it.

"Pssssst." The noise was deliberate.

Turning around, Kimberly knew instinctively who was making it. *Christopher! Christopher!* Uncertainty fueled her frustration until her eyes lit upon a brightly painted playwagon at the upper end of the courtyard.

The sides were paneled, the semicircular top covered with characteristic ornamentation both inside and out to attract attention. It was much like a house on wheels. The rounded top was made of painted canvas stretched over wooden hoops. The back had two large hinged doors for easy loading and unloading, and the front was open, with curtains drawn across to give a small measure of privacy.

The wagon! That was where Christopher was hiding. It was their only chance of escape. All that was needed were the horses, a chore Kimberly intended to see to at once, while the men were so distracted by their search for Christopher they paid no attention to her.

"Hurry! I must hurry!" she told herself.

Never had any task seemed to take so long. In as short a span of time as she could manage, however, the horses were harnessed and ready for travel. Stealthily she pushed aside the curtains. Talking to Christopher's darkened silhouette, she assured him that all would be well, although she wasn't really certain of her promise. They might both be caught and suffer the consequences.

"Never!" she breathed. Somehow she would outwit their pursuers.

Alas, her words were all too soon put to the test. Angry voices and the shuffling of feet warned Kimberly that a group of men were headed toward the wagon. Without even taking another breath Kimberly jumped up and took the reins. Soon the wagon was bouncing and creaking as it moved down the bumpy road.


The wind brought a stinging mist to Kimberly's cheeks and hands as she held tightly to the reins. Indeed, only her fortitude and courage enabled her to endure the long and tiring journey. She had a strong will, and certain that she could bear even the harshest conditions, she was determined not only to save Christopher but to leave her old life behind. Kimberly Bowen was dead. In her place a whole new woman would be resurrected.

"I'll go to London with Christopher. I'll be an actress!"

That was her fondest dream, not only because she would be with him but because she could make a name for herself. She could be somebody, not just a poor relative dependent on charity for every crust of bread.

During the days of Cromwell's Puritan reign the theaters had been closed, but now that Charles II had taken the throne the theater was flourishing. Kimberly remembered Christopher telling her that women now appeared on the stage, unlike the days of William Shakespeare when only males could make a life in the theater. And after all, how difficult could acting be?

"I can do it! I will do it!"

"Do what?" Climbing up to take his turn at the reins, Christopher cast her an inquisitive look.

"Anything I set my mind on," Kimberly explained, suddenly aware that life was not so much what happened to a person but how someone accepted their circumstances. A person could either see the flowers or the weeds. She was determined to view her life from the perspective of the good things that happened and to forget the bad. Since there was no turning back, she saw no purpose in "what if's" or "what might have beens." She had to accept her life just the way it had turned out and hope for the best.

"Then wish you well," Christopher replied. He gave her hand a squeeze. "In case I haven't said it before, I am grateful to you for saving my life, Kimberly."

"It was the least I could do after your fighting for my honor." She smiled shyly, wanting to tell him then and there that loving him had been her main motivation, but she didn't. There would be a better place and time for such a declaration.

"But what about you? Do you have any other relatives? Anywhere to go?"

She shook her head. "No. At least none that I am aware of. As you heard my uncle proclaim, I am bastard born. My father was never married to my mother. I have never had any contact at all with my father's people."

A shadow crossed his brow. "Then where are you going?"

Kimberly answered simply. "With you."

"With me?" He grew sullenly silent. For just a moment her answer had put up a wall between them.

*No. I do not want a woman tagging along with me She is lovely, courageous and desirable, but I do not want to lose my freedom.*

He knew what could happen when you let a woman into your life. She'd change the way you looked, the way you lived and soon even the way you thought. It was much like putting a harness on one of the horses that pulled his wagon. Well, that was not for him. He loved women, enjoyed being with them, but he had never allowed one into his life with any permanency. And yet, what could he do? This woman had probably saved him from hanging. He couldn't just desert her along the road. Or could he?

"I want to be an actress. Like all the beautiful women who bedeck the arm of the king." Her eyes glittered with hope. "I want that more than anything, Christopher." More than anything except for wanting him.

"Hmmm . . ." For the moment at least he was trapped. Unless he wanted to look like the world's worst cad, he had to give in to her whims, at least for the moment.

"Christopher . . . ?"

He shrugged. "Acting is not as easy as you might think. It takes talent and hard work."

"Work?" She laughed bitterly. "Forsooth, thanks to my uncle I know all about that . . . ." As she remembered her uncle's tragic fate she shivered.

Christopher tried to dissuade her. "An actress must have the right timbre in her voice, a sense of timing, poise and grace. She must . . ." He sighed. What was the use? There was just no way to make her understand.

"I can do it. You will see. . . ."

As the days passed she was determined to prove to Christopher that she had an inner strength. Moreover she had it in mind not only to change her attitude but her looks as well.

Just like the actresses, she would coat her eyelashes and eyebrows with charcoal to darken them, she would put pink on her lips and cheeks.

And her name?

As they traveled on the road Kimberly thought about it. Elizabeth. Anne. Juliet. Eve? No. Too common. Too plain.

Glancing over at Christopher, she thought about how wonderful it would be to wear lace, silk and velvet.

"Velvet!"

It brought to mind elegance, beauty. It was a name that was perfect for her purposes. Perfect for her.

# Five

Oh, how good it was to be away from the inn! There were no wooden walls surrounding her, no floors to mop, no patrons to serve. The air was fresh and clean, with no smell of ale. The jingle of the harness and the rumble of the wagon wheels was music to Kimberly's ears. Though she didn't know exactly where they were headed, she didn't really care. She would have gladly gone anywhere with Christopher.

Before them was a beautiful view of rolling hills and well-painted cottages. The early morning crowing of barnyard roosters, the squealing of pigs, the mooing of cows awaiting their milking and the awakening calls of birds, the rich scents on the air made it obvious that they were in the country.

Some of the cottages seemed deserted, but soon the country folk were up and about, like so many ants in an anthill going about their daily chores, even waving at Kimberly and Christopher when they read the letters on the wagon as it passed by. Large horses with strong necks and flaring nostrils were soon hard at work pulling plows, wagons or other farm equipment.

"Look! Look how excited they are to see us." Christopher was flattered and amused. "It will be even better when we reach the towns. Why only the King gets more attention!"

"Perhaps not even he," Kimberly said. Looking at him from beneath her thick lashes, she let her gaze run over him, remembering what it was like to be crushed against the broad strength of his chest, to have his lips upon her own. Stunned by such bold thoughts, she hastily looked away, putting such amorous yens from her mind as she concentrated upon the road.

In truth, Christopher had been modest when he'd told her of an actor's esteem, for as they traveled they were welcomed with open arms. During those nights when no inn was within sight, Christopher managed to secure invitations from farmers or their wives to stay the night; then it was off on the road again.

"We're getting closer and closer all the time," Christopher informed her early one morning. "Are you anxious?"

As they traveled along, getting nearer and nearer to London, the rumble of other wagons could be heard even before they were sighted. It wouldn't be long now. "Merry-go-up, of course so."

Oh, yes, she was anxious to reach their destination, yet at the same time sad to see their journey end. Being with him on the road was so pleasant, so enthralling, that in some ways she would have been content to travel on and on and on. Moreover, Christopher had acted like a true gentleman, so much so that were she to admit it, Kimberly would have had to say she was disappointed. She wanted him to kiss her again, to look upon her with passion's eye.

She had thought about London all along the road, going over and over in her mind just what would happen when she got there. Christopher had told her that all actors entered a company on probationary status and learned by watching others. At first she would play "naught but small roles" as he called them, but if her voice was pleasing, and if she quickly memorized her lines, she might well earn a livable wage.

"Money is paid only when the theater is open. Any closure will bring a proportionate loss to all involved," Christopher explained. Was it any wonder then that the entire theatrical company banded together to make every performance a success? "If all goes well, being an actor can be moderately profitable."

"Then thank God for the King." Upon the restoration of the monarchy, the theaters, once closed and prohibited, had been reopened and acting companies had been restored. Christopher informed her that his company was under George Jolly at the Red Bull.

"Which you will see on the 'morrow." He pointed ahead. "Our destination is way down the road." Flicking the reins, he urged the horses to a faster pace. "Meanwhile, we'll stay for the night at that manor, if they let us."

One more night, Kimberly thought. One more night alone with him, then once they arrived in London she would have to share him with all the actors and actresses of the company.

"Will you sleep in the other room again this time?" she asked, lamenting the distance he always seemed to put between them.

"Of course," he answered softly, though he cast her a sideways glance. "I want to make certain that your virtue is safe, even from me."

"My virtue." Kimberly clutched at her skirt, wishing now that she hadn't been so adamant about it in the past. "Christopher . . ."

"Aye . . . ?"

She wanted to tell him then and there how welcome his arms would be, but alas, she lost her nerve. "Never mind," was all she said.

Later that night, however, as Christopher lay awake in the darkness of the stable, shivering against the chill as he swaddled himself in an old woolen blanket, it was he who longed for the warmth of a woman.

"Stubborn fool!" What on earth had possessed him to act like such a noble ass? The woman was lovely and sweet. She was desirable. Why then had he kept at least an arm's length away from the joys her body promised? Was it fear? Fear of caring for a woman far more than he should? Perhaps.

Indeed, this time his stay upon the road was hardly what one might call exciting. Their "host" had fed them table scraps and, despite the cold, had relegated them to the stables, where the groom had made it very clear that come morn he expected them to be gone.

Now, lying awake in the darkness, as Christopher listened to the noises of the animals in the stalls below and to the wind rattling the loose boards of the stable walls, he knew a loneliness he had never felt before. How he longed to have a certain golden-haired woman in his arms, her body pressed into his own, warming him. The very thought of her brought forth tantalizing memories that stoked the embers of his desire.

"Oh, Kim . . ." He was torn by conflicting emotions. One part of him wanted to go to her, make love to her, enjoy to the fullest the moments they had together. Another part listened to the voice inside his head which warned that were he to take her to his bed, he might well find himself bonded to this young woman for life.

"Christopher . . ."

Hearing his name, he turned his head.

"Christopher . . ."

Christopher attuned his hearing to the noises in the stable. It sounded as if she were getting undressed. Well, he hoped she would sleep better than he would this night.

"Christopher. . . ."

The light of the moon provided just enough illumination for him to see her shape as she moved closer. Propping himself up on one elbow he watched as she approached. Then they were staring at each other, two shadows in the dusky darkness.

A knot formed in the pit of Kimberly's stomach. What on earth had possessed her to be so bold? She was tempting fate. Even so, she took a step closer.

For a long moment he merely looked at her, at the way her gown clung to the tantalizing curves and planes of her body. His blood surged wildly through his veins as slowly, sensuously he reached out and took her by the hand. "Come, lie here beside me, if only for a little while." His eyes glittered as they swept over her. "So beautiful." How was he to know that one woman could get under his skin so, taunt his heart so. . . .

Slowly she knelt down, knowing very well what might follow. Did she want that? Aye, she did. Since her uncle's death she had changed in more ways than one. She wanted to taste of life, of laughter, of passion, of love. . . .

He pulled her down beside him. "My sweet country girl. Do you have any idea . . . ?"

The excitement that raced along her spine was very much like fear as she saw the male intent in his eyes. Pure, raw desire. Still she answered "Yes. . . ."

His mouth came down and muffled his name on her lips. The fingers of one hand tangled in her hair as he kissed her with a fierce, sweet fire. Kimberly gave in without protest. Her hands slid up to lock around his neck, drawing him closer. It seemed so long ago that he had kissed her.

"Then how can you do anything else than give in. An actor I may be, but I can no longer pretend that I do not desire you. . . ."

This said, he slid his hands down her back to cup the firm roundness of her buttocks, lifting her ever closer to him. The feel of him, so hard, so strong, was all she wanted in the world. The heat of his body warmed her, aroused her, turning her thoughts into mush.

"You have the most glorious breasts." His hand swept up to close over them, his expertise making them harden with desire.

Sensations tingled inside her, sending her body into a dizzying maelstrom of need. Moving closer to him, she moaned.

"I want you, so much that I can hardly think of anything else," he whispered. "I should have taken you sooner, should have branded you as mine."

Kimberly's pulse quickened at the passion which burned in his eyes. Perhaps the passion between them had been inevitable from the moment she had first seen him in the taproom. Certainly now he was the center of her world. Being in his arms eclipsed any other thought, any other memory.

"If only . . ." He groaned, his mouth roaming freely, stopping briefly at the hollow of her throat, lingering there, then moving slowly downward to the skin of her bare shoulder. He held her against him, his hands spanning her narrow waist.

He regretted so many things in his life. He had done so many things of which he was not proud. There were coaches he had robbed, men he had killed, women he had taken with hardly a thought. Now as he looked down at her face he was struck by her innocence. He felt strangely soiled. As he had said, if only . . .

Murmuring her name again, he buried his face in the silky strands of her hair, inhaling the delicate fragrance of flowers in their luxurious softness. He should keep to his resolve, he told himself. Kimberly Bowen was the kind of woman a man would want to marry, were he the marrying kind. Had he then a right to take from her what she should keep sacred for the man in her future?

"No . . ." He started to move away, but her fingers parted the fragile fabric of her gown. She positioned his hand to once more cup her firm, budding breast.

"My uncle's death taught me how soon death can come. I want to live, Christopher. And love."

His fingers brought forth a tingling pleasure that gave promise of what she craved, and for the first time in her life she felt wanton, aware of her body as she had never been. Deep inside her was the inborn need to belong to him, to be his lover. And then? Alas, she didn't even want to think of that, of anything past this moment.

It seemed his hands were everywhere, touching her, setting her body afire with the pulsating flame of desire. Kimberly writhed beneath him, giving herself up to the glorious sensations he was igniting within her as he slipped the gown from her shoulders and let it slide slowly down. When at last she was naked, her long blond hair streaming down her back, he looked at her for a long while, his face flushed with passion, his breath a deep-throated rasp.

"You are so lovely!" he murmured, putting his thoughts into words. His hands moved along her back, sending shivers of pleasure through them both, he in the touching and she in being touched. Her waist was small, her breasts perfection, her legs long and shapely. As she stood bathed in moonlight, he let his eyes roam over her body.

Kimberly made no effort to hide her curves from his piercing gaze. Gone was her maidenly modesty. It was her fate, her destiny, to belong to this man. She knew that in every bone, every muscle, every sinew of her body.

"Kim . . ." He spoke her name softly, caressingly. As he touched her she gloried in the thought that her body pleased him, her pulse quickening at the passion which burned in his eyes.

Their kisses were tender at first, but the sparks of their desire soon burst into flame. Desire flooded his mind, obliterating all reason. He had been a gentleman all this time, had left her untouched, but B'God he couldn't be so noble forever. As she had said, time was much too fleeting, happiness all too precarious a pleasure. He wanted her, she wanted him; it was as simple a thing as that.

His mouth moved upon hers, pressing her lips apart, his tongue, exploring gently as she responded, shifting her weight and rolling closer into his embrace.

Oh, blessed Christ, Christopher thought. She fit against him so perfectly, her gentle curves melting against his hard body. It was as though Kimberly had been made for him. Perhaps she had been. Certainly at this moment it seemed so.

"I want no other woman, only you can fill my heart . . ." he whispered against her mouth. He kissed the corners of her lips, tracing their outlines with his tongue, then parting them and seeking the sweetness he knew to be within. His hands moved on her body, stroking her lightly—her throat, her breasts, her

belly, her thighs. With reverence he finally positioned them on
her breasts, caressing gently. Slowly. Until they swelled in his
hands. He outlined the rosy-peaked mound with his finger,
watching as the velvet flesh hardened. Her responding moan
excited him, but he wanted to be gentle, he wanted to make it
beautiful for her, wanted to be the perfect lover. Nevertheless
it took all his self-control to keep his passion in check.

Christopher lingered over her, exploring her with hands and
mouth, discovering the sweetness of her body. His exploration,
like a hundred feathers, was everywhere upon her skin arousing in her a deep, aching longing. Kimberly closed her eyes
to the rapture. Without even looking at him she could see his
strong body, his bold smile, and again thought what a handsome man he was. Yet it was something far stronger that drew
her to him, the gentleness that merged with his strength. Even
though she was new to this matter of passion, she knew instinctively that he was concerned with her pleasure.

Wanting to bring him the same sensations that she was feeling, Kimberly touched him, one hand slipping down over the
muscles of his chest, sensuously stroking the warmth of his
flesh in exploration. She heard his audible intake of breath,
and that gave her the courage to continue in her quest.

"Kim . . . ! He held her face in his hands, kissing her eye-
lids, the curves of her cheekbones, her mouth. "Kim. Kimberly." He repeated her name over and over again as if to taste
of it on his lips.

"I want to please you. . . ." Her fingertips roamed over his
shoulders and neck, plunged into his thick hair as he kissed
her once again, a fierce joining of mouths that bespoke his
passion. In the beauty of his masculinity he towered over her,
so very male.

For a moment Kimberly had second thoughts as she
glimpsed his elongated hardness but Christopher's soothing
words told her he would turn his strength into tenderness and
love. "I like the feel of your skin against me," he breathed,
putting her at ease.

Shattered by the all-consuming pleasure of lying naked beside him, she entwined her arms around his muscled neck, her body writhing in a slow, delicate dance. A heat arose within her as she arched against him in sensual pleasure and her breath became heavier, a hunger for him, like a pleasant pain, racing from her breasts down to her loins. That pulsing, tingling sensation increased as his hand ran down the smoothness of her belly to feel the softness nestled between her thighs.

Kimberly now gave way in wild abandon, moaning intimately, joyously as her fingers likewise moved his body, and a strange sensation flooded over her, one she could not deny.

Gently he kissed her breasts, running his tongue over their tips until she shuddered with delight. Whispering words of love, he slid his hands between her thighs to explore their soft inner flesh. At his touch a slow quivering began deep inside her, becoming a fierce fire as he moved his fingers against her.

Supporting himself on his forearms, he moved between her legs. Slowly he caressed her thigh with his pelvis, letting her get accustomed to the hardness of his maleness.

"Love me, Christopher," she breathed out. "Make me forget everything. . . ." The loneliness, the heartache. Arching up, she was eager to drink fully of that which she had only partially experienced.

"Everything but me. . . ." His mouth closed over hers in hard, fierce possession, his breath mingling with hers, his tongue probing her mouth as he entered her softness with a slow but strong thrust. He pulled her more fully beneath him and buried his length within her sheath, allowing her to adjust to his sudden invasion. She was so warm, so tight around him that he closed his eyes, in almost agonized pleasure.

"My God!" he muttered hoarsely. He wondered how he could ever have thought anything as important as this. At the moment he wanted only to bring her pleasure. If his heart went out to her, then so be it.

As they came together, spasms of feeling wound through Kimberly like the threads of her embroidery. She had never realized how incomplete she had felt until this moment. Now, joined with him, she was a whole being. Feverishly she clung to him, her breasts pressed against his chest. Their hearts beat in matching rhythm even as their mouths met, their tongues entwined, their bodies embraced in the slow sensuous dance of love. Consumed by his warmth, his hardness, she clasped her legs around his waist as she arched up to him, moving in time to his rhythm. He was slow and gentle, taking incredible care of her.

"Christopher . . . !" She clutched at him. It was as if he had touched the very core of her. In an explosion of rapture, their bodies blended into one. Ecstasy. "Love," such a simple word and yet in truth it meant so much. She had never realized how incomplete she had been without him until this moment. With her hands, her mouth, the movements of her body she tried to tell him so, declaring her love with every gesture.

Christopher groaned, giving himself up to the exquisite sensation of flesh sheathing the entire length of him. Again and again he made her his own, wanting to blend his flesh with hers, to bring her the ultimate pleasure of love, succeeding beyond his wildest expectations. With Kimberly Bowen he knew the shattering satisfaction of being whole, of being totally, unselfishly one with a woman. Though he had thought to brand her his, he wondered if, to the contrary, she hadn't placed a mark of possession upon his heart.

Languidly they came back to reality, lying together in the aftermath of passion, their hearts gradually resuming normal rhythms. Time drifted past yet they were reluctant to move and break the spell. Christopher gazed down upon her face, gently brushing back the tangled golden hair from her eyes.

"Sleep now," he whispered, still holding her close. With a sigh, she snuggled up against him, burying her face in the warmth of his chest.

# Six

The first cock's crow awakened Christopher. Opening his eyes, he was reminded all too jarringly that morning had come. He sat up, remembering what had happened during the night, aware that he had discovered feelings he hadn't even known he possessed, conscious that she had touched his heart. Kimberly Bowen made him wish for so many things, inspired so many dreams in him. And yet . . .

Instantly he knew that he had made a terrible mistake. Why hadn't he heeded his common sense? How could he have allowed himself to give in to the passion of the moment?

Looking down at her sleeping face with its veil of golden hair, he felt strangely trapped, frightened. The devil damn him for a fool! He had let himself fall in love! What now?

For a long agonizing moment he sat as still as stone, watching her, wanting her, stunned by how important another person could suddenly become. He wanted to be with her, share all her dreams, follow her to the ends of the earth if it came to that. He wanted a vine-covered cottage, much like the ones they had passed on the way, with children out playing in the yard. He wanted—

"A ring in my nose. . . ." An end to his wandering ways. He had always been a man in search of adventure. It was as if he had Gypsy blood driving him on.

Kimberly. She was the soft spot in his armor. He'd always been a loner but now she inspired dangerous thoughts.

Thoughts he forced from his head. No. He wasn't the kind for marriage, he'd always said that. But leave her? He closed his eyes to the twinge of pain that thought caused. Could he really be that big a bastard? You have to be, a voice answered inside his head.

But what about taking her with him as she had originally planned? That thought played over and over again in Christopher's mind. He'd seen the enthusiasm, the excitement on her face at the thought of joining the theater company. He could find a place for her in it.

*Take her along with him to be his mistress?* That thought turned to ashes in Christopher's mouth. Was that what Kimberly deserved? Was that what he wanted for her? A woman traipsing after her lover as they made the rounds from town to town. A wanderer. A nomad. A woman without a permanent home.

Reaching out he started to brush the hair out of her face, then drew back his hand as if he had been burned. He wasn't ready for this. Perhaps he never would be. But Kimberly was. She deserved more. She was the kind of woman who would make some man a very good wife. Some man. The right man. She needed a protector, someone whose armor wasn't tarnished. As it was he had been highwayman, soldier, philanderer, womanizer. Hardly the type of man to pick up a plow and settle down to a country squire's way of life. And yet . . .

Christopher was conscious of her with every nerve in his body. He hesitated. You decide, he said to himself. Either walk away now or become permanently ensnared. As difficult as it was to think about, it wasn't going to become any easier. The longer he stayed, the harder it would be to leave. And he had to go.

"God's blood!"

*"Kimberly . . ."* Her name escaped from his lips in a breathless gasp. He had to do it. For her welfare much more than his own. They were just too different. For all her hard work, Kimberly had been sheltered from the harsher realities. Life

among the actors would bring these upon her with crushing blows.

"I have to say goodbye. I have to make her understand." Once again he reached out. Perhaps if he woke her, perhaps if he explained . . . But no! He couldn't bear to see the awareness of betrayal in her eyes, or to see her tears. If he did, he would weaken.

Every muscle in Christopher's body stiffened as it suddenly came to him just what he must do. There was no time to lose. He had to depart now, before he changed his mind.

"I'll leave her a large pouch of money, a generous sum she can use for her dowry."

He'd also leave behind a letter telling Kimberly goodbye as gently as he could. Pray God that he could think of the right things to say, he whose living had been made by writing and espousing flowery lines. Goodbye. Such a sad word and yet it needed very much to be said. That and I'm sorry.

Christopher hesitated again, staring at her peacefully sleeping. For a moment he almost changed his mind, almost thought to give their love a chance, anything to ease this aching in his heart. But no! Once again he decried his profession. Life in the theater was not the kind of life for a decent, loving woman. He would hurt her, and if he did not, then the others would.

"Forgive me!" Perhaps when all was said and done, she should have left him to the mercy of the angry crowd at the inn. She had saved his life, had given him her virtue, and now he was leaving, vanishing as silently and as quickly as the wind.

Christopher . . . Christopher! Just the whisper of his name on her lips made Kimberly's heart sing as she awakened. Never had she known such happiness. She had given him her whole heart because she was incapable of holding feelings in reserve, had granted him all her love, her strength, her devotion. I'm his woman, she thought, his lover.

Craving the warmth of his body, she reached for him, only to find herself alone. In disappointment she turned over on her side, her eyes searching for him. He was gone!

"Christopher?"

She smiled. How like him to be up and about at the first sign of morning. Undoubtedly he was harnessing the horses to the playwagon, anxious to be on the way to London.

"London!" Reaching that destination now seemed even more thrilling. They would be in London together. Together.

She sensed that Christopher Sheldon's life had been anything but perfect. A combination of disappointment and cruelty had made him a loner, a man who lived on the edge of danger. He had known coldness, hardship and pain before erecting that thick shell of bravado around himself. Sometimes to stay alive he had been forced to live by his wits and his strength. Kimberly wanted to heal him with tenderness and the soft, burning, worship of her body. She wanted to protect him, to keep him safe.

Quickly she rose from the pile of straw that had been their bed. She hurried to get dressed, humming as she did so. Bending over, she picked up her clothing which was scattered about as Christopher had left it. Slipping into her chemise and petticoat, she pulled at the drawstring at the waist, allowing herself to dream. Kimberly Sheldon! The two names fit so perfectly together. Would it ever be? Would Christopher ask her to marry him? She had to believe that he would, for the thought of his ever leaving her was decidedly painful. Indeed, it was so troubling that she put it from her mind as she hurried to dress. It wouldn't do to dally. She had to get ready so that when he returned they could be on their way.

But he didn't return. Hurrying to the stable, she looked out. The wagon was gone!

"No!" Pressing her hands to her temples, she refused to even contemplate what that could mean. He must have moved the wagon, that was all. Aye, he had driven it over to the manor house so that he could say his thank you's to the master, even if the man didn't deserve such courtesy.

Pacing up and down, she almost wore a hole in the floor, waiting, waiting waiting. Time passed, he didn't return. There was no sign of him.

"Christopher!" Cupping her hands to her mouth she cried out his name. Alas, there was no human response. Only the sounds of the birds, the horses and the rooster disturbed the silence of the morning. "Dear God!" Sometime while she had slept he had left.

"How could he?" Tears stung her eyes. Disappointment and heartache threatened to choke her. Knowing that she had been left behind without even a second thought nearly destroyed her. Then, her sorrow turning to anger, it became a burning rage as hot as the flames of passion he had inspired. All too abruptly her dream world had come to a shattering end.

"No!"

Picking up her skirts, Kimberly ran down the road.

# Part Two:
# The Velvet Temptress
## London

"To hold, as 'twere, the mirror up to nature."

—William Shakespeare, *Hamlet*

# *Seven*

London was a city of loud noises, even in the dark hours of the morning. The clip-clop of horses' hooves, the clattering of coach and wagon wheels against the cobblestones; the loud voices of rosy-cheeked milkmaids and of the sellers of newly gathered cresses shattered the illusion the soft glow of the lanterns cast upon the roadway. Surrounded by a medieval wall, London was a jumbled, cluttered city as the early morning light would soon reveal. Gabled houses were crammed together, furtive types haunted alleyways that teemed with criminals, yet this was the place that Christopher more often than not called home.

"Strange how this city now seemed so lonely, so desolate, despite the people."

His head ached, his throat felt dry, his conscience pricked him at every turn. It all will pass, he told himself, but that didn't help. Perhaps the worst was still to come. Why hadn't he realized what a terrible toll guilt could take on a man? he asked himself. Why hadn't he perceived how difficult it would be?

Turning his head he clutched at the reins, tempted to go back. Would Kimberly still be there? No. He had been traveling a day and a night. It was too late. Undoubtedly by now she was gone, hopefully back to the inn.

She would be all right there. The citizens had had time to cool their tempers. They would now be thinking about what had happened. Besides, it was he who had wielded the sword, not Kimberly. She would not be blamed. Perhaps she could start her life anew, marry a fine upstanding citizen of the town. At the worst she would most likely take control of her uncle's tavern. Certainly she, of all women, could make it prosper.

The Thames glittered like brass in the moonlight as the play-wagon rattled across London bridge. It was still dark at this early hour. Most Londoners were still abed, and those upon the streets seemed to pay little attention to the wagon.

"The Black Unicorn," Christopher whispered. The wooden sign decorated with the painted mythological beast proclaimed that he had reached his destination. Here he was to meet the others of his company. Richard Fletcher, William Dryden, Anthony Marlowe. He was eager for them to read his new play.

One of the main problems facing theater companies now that the theater was alive again was the acquisition of a suitable repertory, not that Shakespeare's plays weren't still viable. They were. It was just that they had been around so long, some thought them a little old-fashioned, though many of his works had been revised to bring them into line with the day.

Love versus honor. This was the theme of popular plays. Thinking about it Christopher cringed. Love. Honor. Surely he had betrayed them both.

With a cry of anger, he twisted the reins, so hard he hurt his fingers. He would not think of *her.* He would put her out of his heart, out of his mind. What was done was done. All for the best in the long run. He would busy himself with the company, B'God, there were certainly enough problems to be solved. A theater for one. The Red Bull had been used for a short time following the Restoration, but some in the company thought it not sufficiently suited to Italianate scenery.

"Nay, we might well have to find another place so that we can be competitive with the other acting companies in London." There were the players at the Drury Lane Theatre and those of the Lincoln's Inn Fields Theater, which had been converted from Lisle's Tennis Court. Christopher swore beneath his breath. Since the time of Shakespeare, theaters were becoming larger and more elaborate.

As Christopher alighted from the wagon he visualized the interior of a theater. The auditorium was divided into pit, boxes and gallery. Unlike the French, the English pit was raked to improve sight lines and was equipped with backless benches for all spectators. There were two or sometimes even three galleries. The first was partitioned into boxes while the uppermost remained open. The middle gallery, if indeed the theater had one, was divided between boxes and an open area.

"Well, we shall see. We shall see."

He pulled open the tavern's portal. The interior of the Black Unicorn was dimly lit. The fire in the hearth had burned to embers, only a few candles illuminating the room. Even so, Christopher noticed the man standing in the corner of the tavern immediately. "Richard!"

The man's eyes sparkled with gladness at seeing him. "We've missed you, Christopher. As a matter of fact you were gone so long, some of us feared you might have taken to the highways again." Pointing his finger, he mocked good-naturedly, "Stand and deliver." It was the command highwaymen delivered when accosting victims.

"Stand and deliver indeed, you old pirate." Christopher was not the only one who had a notorious past.

"So, what were you about all the time you were gone?"

Christopher studied his friend as he related the details of his play, a romance he believed to be as finely wrought as *Romeo and Juliet*.

Richard Fletcher was older than Christopher, in his mid-thirties. Of average height and build, he dressed in garments that were fashionable but somber, unlike those of most men who shared his profession. His brown hair was worn nearly to his shoulders. A hairline which was beginning to recede made him appear much older than his years. As was the style, he wore a mustache and clipped beard.

"Ah, it sounds as if you have written romantic prose." Richard winked. "Was it based upon experience, Chris? Did you find some fair country girl with whom to trifle?"

Christopher cringed at the reminder. "No!" he answered curtly.

"If you remained celibate all the while that in itself would make an interesting story." Throwing back his head, Richard Fletcher gave in to his mirth. "Ah, Chris, Chris! What are we to do with you?"

"What am I to do with myself!" Christopher leaned against the wall, frowning. Oh, why was it so difficult to forgive himself for what he had done? Why was it so hard to forget? Kimberly . . . Where was she now? What was she doing?

Kimberly might well have returned to Reedham. Instead, she was at this moment trudging along the road. If she had to walk all the way to London, that was just fine! She would, however, get there. She was going to be an actress. She was! The determination had become an obsession.

She held her breath in anticipation, refusing to notice how painful her feet were. Blisters. She knew she had those in abundance. Still, she would not turn back. She was going to be an actress if it killed her!

Velvet Tremaine. The name stuck in her head. She would become the talk of London, a beauty to rival them all. Then let Christopher repent of his actions.

How loathsome he had been! How cruel. In her heart she knew she would never forgive him for what he had done. And if that hadn't been bad enough, he had left her a sackful of money, as if to cleanse himself of his deed. Or as if her virtue had a price. But she would make him sorry. Somehow they would meet again. She would make him fall in love with her, and then she would leave him as he had left her. Somehow . . .

Engrossed in her dream, immersed in thoughts of revenge for what he had done, she did not hear the horse's hooves until the creature was nearly upon her.

"God's teeth!" Only by the greatest of efforts was the horseman able to avoid her.

"Ah . . . !"

Quickly dismounting, the rider approached her, making certain that she was all right. Giving in to his curiosity, he questioned her. "What is a beauty like you doing walking along the road?"

"I'm going to London!" she informed him. "To be an actress!"

"An actress?" For just a moment the corners of his mouth inched up in a smile; then he shrugged. "Then perhaps our meeting was meant to be, for I am an actor."

"An actor?" She winced. "Forsooth, not another one!" No doubt they were all alike.

"Ah, such a look." He leaned forward. "Well, no matter what you might think, I am different." He introduced himself. "Jonathan Fairfax, actor extraordinaire. And you?"

"Velvet!" She said it again, liking the sound. "Velvet Tremaine." She had the urge to confide in him, to tell him what had happened, but held herself back. It was too early to trust anyone. Perhaps she never really would again.

He looked puzzled, as if trying to remember her.

"I've never been on the stage, but I am going to be soon." She tossed her head, feigning an assurance she really did not feel.

"Ah. . . ." He pointed toward his horse. As if sensing that she might be in some sort of trouble, he invited her to ride with him. "London is different than the country. You will have need of friends." He promised to teach her all the tricks of the acting profession.

Kimberly was exhausted. Leaning against him as they rode, she fell asleep.

She awakened just as they reached the outskirts of London. Along the gentle curve in the road stood rows of narrow brick houses wall to wall, the stronghold of the middle-class, small shopkeepers, clerics and modest men. Each house had a small fenced green in front, trim curtains and window boxes full of flowers to signal that the owners were no longer of the working class.

There was little activity at this early morning hour, but just on the other side of Newgate, at Smithfield market, a few people were beginning to set up their stalls, so the pair stopped for just a moment to purchase some fresh fruit and vegetables to eat along the way.

"We have actors aplenty in our company, but perhaps we might be able to use you," Jonathan was saying. "We have need of a quick-witted actress who is able to take many short roles. We will give you a chance to show what you can do."

"Thank you. I will be grateful whatever happens." Kimberly couldn't help but wonder what this matter of acting entailed. Surely she could handle it, if need be. How difficult could it possibly be to memorize a few sentences and move about a stage?

"Good. The company will be doing two plays. *MacBeth* and a new play by Roger Boyle, the earl of Orrery. It's called the *Tragedy of Mustapha."* He grinned, gesturing toward the city. "Welcome to London, Velvet."

"London . . ." Sitting up straight she drew in a deep breath. If the air smelled of smoke, garbage and dust, well she just didn't care. She was here. She had arrived. But this was just the beginning. . . .

# Eight

For the first time in a long, long while Kimberly had the sense of belonging. She was content with her new life among the actors, content in the friendship she had forged with Jonathan Fairfax. True to his word he had taught her a great deal about life in the theater.

"Let's just say that we will learn together," he had insisted. "For there is always much to be learned."

And there was. Never had Kimberly worked so hard. She devoured scripts, saying aloud each line. She practiced her diction. She did in fact live, eat and breathe the theater.

She soon found that everything went according to schedule, including eating and sleeping. Approximately twenty people gathered together for many hours each day.

The theatrical season ran from October to June. Performances were advertised in various ways, generally by posters set about the city and by handbills distributed at coffee houses, private homes and elsewhere.

Rehearsals ran from ten in the morning until one in the afternoon. Performances were at three, but since seats were given to the patrons who arrived first, it was not unusual for people to arrive early or send servants to hold their seats. Seats were unnumbered, so squabbles over them were not unusual.

The theater was a world unto its own as Kimberly was soon to discover. It was a colorful sphere of make-believe and pretense in which for a while reality was put at bay in favor of the fantasies the actors created. Even she was able to forget her heartache as she delved into this new environment. As the others in whose company she found herself, Kimberly was completely absorbed in preparing for and in executing performances. Urged on by Jonathan, who most patiently and skillfully tutored her, she spent the next few weeks dedicating herself to learning her lines in the hope that she could at least manage her appearances reasonably well.

Acting was not as easy as she had first supposed, not by any means. It was much more than memorizing lines and phrases and repeating them. It was portraying a character in detail and so convincingly that all who looked on believed in the creations. Gestures, tone of voice, movement—all added to the performance and defined novice from professional.

Some of the men she traveled with had been trained from childhood in this profession, and had even risked punishment to perform during the years of the Commonwealth and the Protectorate when theater performances were forbidden. These daring men had often acted in the short farcical plays that had been dubbed "drolls."

"The theater was in our blood. We couldn't give it up," Jonathan said of his friends. "We all believed in our hearts that it would be legalized again. We knew Cromwell couldn't last, that he would come tumbling down."

As for Kimberly's attributes, Jonathan and the others gave her praise. "You have a lithe, graceful body and a good voice; that is to your advantage," he told her.

And he explained the plays were full of action, but in the final analysis it was not the physical activity that held the attention of the crowd but the emotions, the words. Shakespeare knew this, and it is why he wrote such beautiful poetry in his plays.

The late afternoon sun sparkled in the cloudless blue sky, shining on the sea of blossoms covering the trees outside the tavern where the actors were practicing. Birds flew from bough to bough, their singing brilliant and cheerful, but Kimberly scarcely noticed. Her head was so filled with syllables that she feared it would soon burst. Her temples throbbed in an unrelenting ache as she squinted her eyes in Jonathan's direction.

"I haven't had the chance to properly thank you for all you have done," she said softly. "But I am grateful, Jonathan."

She had learned that whenever Jonathan was tongue-tied he grinned. He did so now. Sheepishly. "Welllll . . ."

She returned his grin with one of her own. She was coming to know this man, and with each day that passed, she liked him all the more; for despite his being an actor, there was no artifice with Jonathan. He was what he was and did not pretend. How could she not be charmed by him?

Sequestering himself in the back of the Black Unicorn with her, Jonathan had taken her under his wing, explaining the organization of the group.

"There is always a director of the troupe, called a "captain." For this tour the man in charge was to be Jonathan. "Acting companies are organized on the sharing plan," he'd informed her.

She had learned that the profits as well as the financial risks were divided among the members.

"After each performance the shareholders divide the money left, after meeting all expenses that is. The account books are open for any of the players to see."

Jonathan had gone on to say that the expenses included payments to authors, hired men and the fund out of which the common stock of costumes, properties and other materials was purchased. So far the performances had been quite profitable.

Though not all actors were shareholders, Kimberly followed Jonathan's advice and promptly made an agreement to be one of those who would risk her earnings on the venture. She hoped it would not be long before she was earning a goodly sum.

Jonathan was careful to familiarize Kimberly with the dos and the don'ts of the players. Every company had rules of conduct and fines for their infringement. Kimberly learned that each player was to be fined one shilling for lateness to rehearsals, three shillings for lateness to a performance, ten shillings for being intoxicated during a performance, twenty shillings for missing a performance and forty pounds for taking any company property.

Learning the rules and regulations was just the beginning, however. Mercilessly Jonathan hounded her on the finer points of acting. He tutored her before cockcrow, cornered her every time the company rested and took up every moment of her spare time. Long after the others had retired for the night, she and Jonathan burned the midnight oil, reading and reciting. He was determined to be a stern taskmaster.

I can do it. I will do it, Kimberly kept telling herself.

Acting companies had only one full copy of each play. In this "prompt book," notes were made relating to the performance—cues for sound, music and special effects; entrances and exits; notations about properties. The prompt book was helpful to Kimberly, and gave her an advantage, because the other actors were merely given "sides" which included only their own lines and cues. During the performances a "plot" or skeletal outline of the action indicating entrances, exits, properties, music and the names of the players to be called would be hung up backstage for quick reference.

"So much to remember, Jonathan," Kimberly said again and again. "So very much to think, do and say. All at the same time." Even so, she never gave up, and soon Jonathan's presence had become a beloved habit. He was her dearest friend.

How sad it was that Jonathan wanted more. The memory of Christopher's betrayal was too recent an ache in her heart, and with a sigh of regret, she always pulled away whenever there was the possibility their being together could become amorous.

Jonathan was good at hiding his disappointment, and good-natured about her reaction. "Ah, but you are a lovely challenge! Perhaps someday . . ."

Kimberly didn't answer. At the moment her thoughts were on Christopher. She had seen on a handbill that he was to appear in a performance of *Hamlet,* playing the title role. Oh, Christopher. How long would it take her to forget?

Christopher Sheldon drummed his fingers on the large mahogany desk top, squinting against the dim lighting of the room as he concentrated on the play script that lay spread out before him. He was so close to accomplishing all of his dreams. So close to being recognized, not only as an actor but as a writer with a talent unknown since the days of Shakespeare and Christopher Marlowe after whom he had been named.

*The Tragedy of the Highwayman,* so the title page of the play read. His fingers stroked the letters proudly. It had been a long struggle, but he had proved beyond a doubt that he could make it on his own, that he had no need of his wealthy grandfather's influence. Indeed, he had boldly unleashed the collar from around his neck and launched his own career.

Clutching his pen, Christopher carefully added the finishing details to the drama, based on the exploits of a man he had once deemed a hero, Gentleman James, a dashing, romantic fellow who unfortunately had met his end swinging on Tyburn tree. In the play that dashing highwayman's doings were combined with a few adventures Christopher had experienced himself in his all too brief stay on the Heath. Ah, but he had fond memories of those days. . . .

"Perfect!" There was no trace of modesty in his tone as he whispered the word to himself. Indeed, he was the sort of man who knew his worth and saw no reason to hide it. It was a lesson his teacher, Michael Mohun of Killigrew's famous acting company, had taught him. " 'All the world's a stage,' " Mohun had said, quoting Shakespeare. With so many people babbling, he'd added, a smart man kept his silence, studying the others all the while. Once he had something to say, however, he said it loudly, distinctly and with a flair. That was the way to get noticed.

"Ah, there you are, sequestered in your cage like a bear before baiting?" Christopher's thoughts were interrupted as the door flew open and Richard Fletcher stepped briskly into the room.

Christopher scowled at the comparison, not having a liking for the gambling sport that pitted an animal against a pack of snarling dogs. "I hope you don't infer that you think the audience will be quarrelsome tonight. I am not in the mood."

Richard held up a hand. "Nay, quite the contrary. The whole of London is looking forward to our revised version of Shakespeare's antiquated play. They have even suggested that we have a parade."

"A parade?" Christopher smiled at the thought of such adulation.

"For which I am glad, if it will serve to improve the foul mood you have been in of late." Richard stared in an effort to read Christopher's thoughts. "Something has been troubling you. How I do wish you would tell. I am your friend, you know."

"I know." It was just that Christopher didn't want to even think about Kimberly Bowen, much less talk about her. She was too great a prick to his conscience.

Sensing that his friend was not going to open up to him, Richard changed the subject. "Are you nearly finished?"

"I am!" Christopher crumpled up a piece of paper and tossed it at the wastebasket with a shout of glee.

"Let me see." Plopping down into a leather chair, Richard sprawled out comfortably. Snatching up the thick stack of paper, he scanned it hastily. "Mmmm, adventuresome. Romantic." Many of the recent plays had an emphasis upon love versus honor in the style of the French and Spanish authors. "Funny at times."

"And true. . . ."

"But pray, such a sad ending." The play ended with the

death of Gentleman James amidst the tearful sobbing of his daughter, likewise a character in the play. "If I were you I would change to a happy ending."

Christopher grimaced as he remembered watching the highwayman swing. "Happy? How? The man was most grievously betrayed by Scar, one of his own and all on account of rivalry and jealousy. How then make it happy?"

Richard sounded like a schoolmaster lecturing one of his boys. "Contrive a happy ending. Else we will hear about it from the crowd."

"Who will hoot and holler if they are annoyed by my clever prose." Christopher was stubborn. "No. I write this as a tribute to James and to all who were so betrayed by Cromwell and his ilk. The ending stands." He could see by the expression on Richard's face that his friend just wouldn't understand. "I suppose it is impossible to right the injustices in the world. But perhaps I can at least make certain they are not forgotten."

Richard looked at Christopher, then suddenly pounded him on the back. "That's the old Christopher Sheldon I know so well. A man who will spit in the eye of conformity at his own risk." His voice grew soft as he inquired, "But do tell, what will you do if there are those who ask how you have such intimate knowledge of life on the roads?"

Christopher tapped his head. "I will tell them I am a man of great imagination."

# Nine

A visit from King Charles himself could not have been received with more enthusiasm than was shown the actors as they paraded down the street, leading the citizens of London to the theater. Voices rose up in shouts, and the sounds of laughter and merriment followed the players down the neatly cobbled street toward the theater.

Young women and old threw flowers at the players until the street was covered with blossoms of red, white, blue and gold, some of them casting come-hither smiles that inferred they were willing to share their favors with any actor so inclined.

Weaving in and out among the crowd, Kimberly made certain there was no chance that Christopher might see her. All the while she wondered what on earth had possessed her to come in the first place. Curiosity?

"I want to see him perform. I want to understand what drives him." Perhaps then, and only then, she could understand why he had left.

The procession passed all the way to Saint James Field, walking down Catherine Street, named in honor of the queen, and heading north to Knightsbridge and beyond. The onlookers twittered in the courtyard expectantly, anxious to get a glimpse of the lead actor. Standing on tiptoe, Kimberly sought a view of him too, ill prepared for the ache in her heart that came when she did see him.

Dressed in his costume for the play, a black velvet suit of

the latest fashion, he looked regal, handsome and inspiring. Costuming for the tragedy was in the style of the garments of the day, thus he wore his hair flowing free to his shoulders, and his mask gave a touch of fantasy to the drama.

"Christopher . . ." Without thinking she reached out to him, only narrowly ducking out of sight as she remembered herself. She didn't want him to see her. Not yet. Not until she had made a name for herself. Instead she would watch carefully from a distance as each player rode by.

Most of those assembled in the procession were just as flamboyantly dressed as Christopher. As they rode past, her eyes sought each one out. There was a tall man dressed all in green, a heavyset man, full of face and with the surly look of a fighter about him, dressed in dark blue; then came the actresses. One dressed in black, her long auburn hair held back from her face with pearls, caught Kimberly's eye. This strikingly beautiful woman kept looking in Christopher's direction as if trying to catch his eye.

"Who is she . . . ?"

"That's the actress who plays Hamlet's sister. Linette Penn," a woman beside Kimberly answered aloud. "They say that all of London is in love with her, including the King."

"Oh . . ." What was the actress to Christopher? Just wondering was painful.

Once again her eyes touched upon the man who had so changed her life. Despite her hurt and her anger, she had to admit he made an extremely romantic figure standing in the bright haze of sunlight, tight black knee pants hugging his long, muscular legs, his black coat straining as he reached out to take flowers from a young admirer's hand.

For just a moment Kimberly felt that her heart would burst. For that moment it was as if they were all alone on the street; then, just as suddenly, the moment was gone. Sadly she watched him ride away.

\* \* \*

The theater was a cacophony of sound. Each part—boxes, pit and galleries—had its own entrance, ticket sellers and ticket takers as well as its own small band of merchants, beggars, traders, mountebanks, peddlers and pickpockets waiting, already taking advantage of the crowds.

"Ale! Wine!" cried out a man selling liquid refreshment. He held up a bottle of ale.

"Oranges. . . ." called out the orange girls. Each girl had a dream-struck look in her eyes, hoping to go on stage someday, or perhaps to catch the fancy of a noble patron.

"Sausages! Hot sausages!" The cry of this seller reminded Kimberly of her hunger. Buying a long sausage and a small cup of ale, she walked along as she ate, then purchased a ticket and took a seat in the box.

The shrill blast of a trumpet made announcement of the play, *Hamlet, Prince of Denmark*. The bill was complex, Jonathan had told her, consisting of the full-length play, with singing and dancing between the acts. Kimberly settled herself in her seat, prepared to spend a long period of time.

Act one opened on a platform set before the castle. As she watched the play unfold, Kimberly took note of each actor's voice and movement, the way each played to the audience. Good actors had what Jonathan called "timing," intuitively sensing when and how to speak lines to best benefit the flow of the play.

As Christopher came upon the stage to say his lines, she knew in a moment that of all the actors he was the one who truly had presence. From the moment he began speaking, he held the audience in his hand.

" ' . . . 'Tis not alone my inky cloak, good mother, nor customary suits of solemn black, nor windy suspiration of forc'd breath. . . .' "

Closing her eyes Kimberly remembered sitting beside him in the playwagon as he'd practiced his lines. Even then she had been spellbound by his voice.

" 'O, that this too too solid flesh would melt, thaw and resolve itself into a dew!' "

Entranced, Kimberly concentrated upon his every expression, his every move. In a corner of her mind she understood that this was where Christopher belonged. Here, on the stage. Indeed, it was this and not another woman that had been her rival. The theater was in his blood, his heart, his soul. It was his love, his life, his mistress. It was here that he had total power, total control over every other being.

When the play began there had been a constantly chattering crowd, a most discourteous throng who seemed to think it their privilege to shout out comments to the actors as if they imagined themselves to be a part of the dramatics. During the times when Christopher was on stage, however, not a sound was heard, not even a cough.

" 'To be, or not to be, . . . that is the question. Whether 'tis nobler in the mind to suffer the slings and arrows of outrageous fortune, or to take arms against a sea of troubles, and by opposing end them? To die, to sleep . . .' "

Only once in the entire performance did he falter, and that was when he looked out at the crowd and his eyes focused on Kimberly. Had he recognized her? She wasn't certain. Perhaps neither was he, for he had a quizzical expression. Hastily she moved her head so that her face was hidden behind the shoulders of the tall man who sat in front of her.

" 'To sleep! perchance to dream, ay, there's the rub, for in that sleep of death what dreams may come when we have shuffled off this mortal coil. . . .' "

From the security of her hiding place Kimberly could see that he looked her way again, no doubt wondering if his eyes had deceived him.

What would he do were we to meet again? How would he act, what would he say. Alas, that she should even care. And yet, it was not an easy thing to turn off feelings. " 'Ay, there's the rub,' " she whispered, quoting one of Hamlet's lines.

The play was long, the seat hard, yet Kimberly had to admit to herself that she had treasured each and every moment. When the performance had ended, when the actors had received their applause and taken their bows, she stood up. In that moment Christopher looked her way again, and this time she knew for certain that she had been spotted.

"Kimberly . . ." She saw him mouth her name, noticed the way he raised his arm as if to reach out to her, and in that moment she knew that the love she felt for him would never die. It was a truth that hit her hard as she fled from the theater.

"Christopher, what's wrong?" Richard Fletcher put a hand upon Christopher's arm.

"Wrong?"

"You look as if you have seen a ghost." Fletcher laughed.

"Perhaps I did." Christopher took a deep breath, trying to calm his heart. It had been her! He had seen her face in the audience, with his very own eyes. She had been there! Or had it been her ghost come back to haunt him.

"The performance is over, man. The ghost is no longer upon the stage to haunt you. . . ."

"Yet I will be haunted nonetheless. . . ." For how was he to have known how hard it would be to forget one woman or one magical moment in time when all the world had quieted for the sake of a kiss?

"Haunted by all the adoring women who seek your attention." Richard's tone held envy.

"Extend my regrets, but I can not dine tonight." Seeing Kimberly's face, even if it had been naught but a vision, had deeply troubled him. "I want to be alone."

"Alone?" Richard was incredulous.

"Alone." He wanted to think, to reflect on his life and where he wanted it to go from here. And Kimberly? He just didn't know, though he had to admit there were times when he'd thought of searching for her, whether in London or in Reedham or wherever she might be.

# Ten

Kimberly was inspired after having seen the performance of *Hamlet* at the Red Bull Theater. Although she had been working hard, she now worked even harder. She wanted to learn to be just as good an actress as Christopher was an actor. With that thought in mind, she forced herself to go on even when she was exhausted. Little by little she was developing self-confidence and becoming determined to put the past behind her and do everything possible to advance her new career.

If every once in a while Jonathan would give himself a pat on the back by suggesting that he had been the one responsible for her ability, it was to be expected, she supposed. He had taught her more things about acting and the theater than she could ever have imagined. Still, at least for the time being, Kimberly's parts had been relegated to walk-ons and unimportant roles. That is, until the actress playing Lady MacDuff fell off the scaffolding and broke her leg.

It was a golden opportunity as Jonathan said, yet Kimberly was unsure of herself and fearful of the situation.

"Jonathan, I'm just not ready." Her hands went cold as if the blood had drained from them. She'd never realized she would feel such fear at the very thought of speaking before the crowds. What if she forgot a line, or moved too far upstage? What if—

"B'God! Of course you are." Jonathan seemed to be attuned

to her emotions. Grasping her hands in his he rubbed them gently between his own, warming them. "You'll be just fine."

"What if my voice doesn't carry over the crowd, what if I suddenly can't remember." It was a worry that always plagued an actor. Practicing was one thing, performing before hundreds of people another.

Jonathan kissed her lightly on the cheek. "You worry too much, my lovely Velvet."

"And for good reason. . . ." She didn't want to make a fool of herself.

"Forsooth, I've seen you, I've listened to you. You are truly an actress born."

It was a compliment she could not ignore. Still, in spite of Jonathan's confidence in her, Kimberly was nervous. As the first touch of anxiety crept over her, she knew she was experiencing what Jonathan and a few of the others always termed "stage fright." Try as she might, her stomach was tied in knots at the very thought of being watched by so many people. The company had poured a great deal of money into the playbills and other advertisements, and record-breaking crowds were expected when the show opened. How then could she not be a nervous wreck.

Posters large enough to cover the entire side of a house were plastered on walls, houses, stores and everywhere in between, all announcing that Shakespeare's *MacBeth* would be performed at Salisbury Court. The playbill listed all the actor's names, announcing the debut of a lovely newcomer to the stage. Velvet Tremaine. The advertisement promised an amazing performance. Was it any wonder then that when the first day of the play came people chattered, howled and shouted in their excitement.

There was a goodly crowd at Salisbury Court, one just as large as had been at the Red Bull to see *Hamlet*. Times were more prosperous for some, and even those upon whom fate had not yet smiled had come to see the players. Hawkers sold tobacco, apples, nuts and pamphlets to the spectators, thus assuring themselves of hefty profits. The theater was noisy, so much so that Kimberly feared she would not be able to think; much less remember.

"It seems our reputation has preceded us, Velvet," the red-haired actor named Percival Perry—he would be playing Mac-Beth—called out as he stretched his solid bulk.

"Aye. Let us hope they are pleased." Kimberly knew by now that there was no counting on decent or orderly behavior from such an audience. She prayed she could remember her part despite the nut-cracking noise, the raucous jokes and the gratuitous contributions of fruits and vegetables from the theatergoers if a performance wasn't to their liking.

"Let's hope." Frowning she looked over at Jonathan who was dressed for his role as one of the three witches, complete with a wig and false nose.

"It looks as if the ale has been flowing freely." He sniffed. It smelled like it too. "Well then, it seems the crowd will be in a relaxed mood."

Pushing through the crowd, Kimberly headed for the tiring-house to change. Hers was to be a dark green gown with low décolletage, lace collar and full sleeves. Since time and place were deemed unimportant most characters wore contemporary garments, thus her gown was one in the latest style. She adjusted the bodice, then put a long, dark-haired wig upon her head. Securing it to her own hair, she tossed her head back and forth to make certain the wig would not fall off while she was upon the stage.

As to the sets, wings, borders and shutters were the standard units. Sets were anonymous and could be used in many different plays. They would be shifted by means of grooves installed on the stage floor and overhead. Upon a whistled signal from the prompter, stagehands would make all the necessary changes. The front curtain would be raised after the Prologue and not lowered until the end of the performance, thus all changes were made in full view of the audience.

"Once this all begins there will be little place to hide. . . ." So thinking, she was tentative as she left the tiring-house.

"Ah, Velvet. . . ." James Nokes whose specialty was playing old husbands, clumsy fops and ridiculous old women greeted her. Like Jonathan he would be playing a witch, a role deemed more suitable for men.

"Lord, she is a beauty. She will astound them. After the performance she will undoubtedly be the talk of all London!" Charles Hart, whose facial expressions were dramatic even when he was not on the stage, had been chosen to play MacDuff and thus her husband. With a smile he dubbed her "my lady."

Jonathan winked, then hurried on the stage to begin his scene amidst thunder and lightning. " 'When shall we three meet again in thunder, lightning, or in rain?' "

" ' . . . Fair is foul and foul is fair; hover through the fog and filthy air.' "

Kimberly took a deep breath. It wouldn't be long now, for she had learned that when one was to step upon a stage the time flew by. Christ's mercy, please don't let me have a lapse of memory now. If that happened she knew she would never have the courage to step upon the stage again. Never!

*MacBeth* was a tale of murder and betrayal wherein a king was murdered for the sake of ambition. MacDuff, being MacBeth's antagonist, was endangered and forced to flee. In order to wipe out all those of his line, his wife and children were set upon. Though the part of Lady MacDuff was not huge, it was an important role, the climax of which came near the end of the play. Only because of this was Kimberly able to relax a bit, watching from the sidelines as the drama enfolded.

Much sooner than she could have anticipated the scene switched to a room in MacDuff's castle, where three murderers had been sent to carry out their terrible deed. Kimberly swept onto the stage, quickly gathering her courage and her poise. She would be a success!

" 'What had he done, to make him fly the land?' " she asked about her husband, MacDuff.

" 'You must have patience, madam,' " the actor facing her responded.

For just a moment Kimberly's mind went blank, then like the refrain of a familiar song her lines returned to her. " 'He had none. His flight was madness, when our actions do not, our fears do make us traitors.' "

" 'You know not whether it was his wisdom or his fear.' "

She thought about Christopher and poured her heart into her lines. " 'Wisdom! To leave his wife, to leave his babes, his mansion and his titles, in a place from whence himself does fly? He loves us not. He wants the natural touch; for the poor wren, the most diminutive of birds, will fight, her young ones in her nest, against the owl. All is the fear, and *nothing* is the love. . . .' "

Much to her relief and delight, Kimberly finished her scene without any flaws. Having witnessed the troubling death of her uncle, she was caught up in emotion during the scene in which Lady MacDuff witnessed the murder of her son. At that moment the death was real. She was reliving a killing.

"Murder!" she cried out. Then she was exiting after the death of her stage son, fleeing from the murderers just as surely as she had run from the townsmen of Reedham. God help her if they ever followed.

"Bravo!" Jonathan whispered in praise. "You have earned respect this day. From now on every man in London will wonder who you are."

What Jonathan said was true. Though he only caught a glimpse of the new dark-haired actress, Christopher knew in an instant that she was beautiful. Fascinating. But it was much more than that. She had a certain quality that set her apart from other women. He would have to tell the others that this rival theater company might well give them some stiff competition, in particular because of the young woman's appeal.

"Who is she . . . ?" Something bothered him about her appearance, something he just couldn't put his finger on. As he elbowed his way through the onlookers when the performance was over, Christopher was clearly intrigued.

# *Eleven*

All of London was talking about the new actress who had entered upon the scene. Gossip traveled fast it seemed. Kimberly was a success! Handbills and pamphlets spoke of the unusually attractive dark-haired actress who had given such a brief but poignant performance. The Velvet Temptress, they proclaimed her.

Jonathan was quick to take advantage of the city's mood. "Ah yes, Kimberly has most certainly proven herself. Seems to me she deserves a lot more than the pittance you said you would pay her." He winked at Kimberly. "And much larger parts," he suggested. "How about Katharina in *The Taming of the Shrew?*" With himself as Petruchio of course. Richard would be perfect as Lucentio and Rhiamon Barry as Bianca.

It was one of Jonathan's faults of character that he was greedy. Moreover there when times when Kimberly sensed he was using her success to further himself. And yet, why not? Were it not for him she might well be selling oranges instead of receiving such acclaim.

"I'd say if you had the intelligence of a goose, you'd double her earnings, just to make certain she doesn't run off." Putting his hands on his hips, Jonathan declared. "And mine as well."

William's eyebrows furled, his gray eyes darted fire. "B'God, but I never realized that you were so greedy."

"Well, I am! A man," he turned toward Kimberly, "and a woman have to know their worth."

William's oath was a deep rumble. "She has given one performance, B'God. She is still untried." For just a moment Kimberly feared he might tell both her and Jonathan to go to the devil, but then his furled brows became two straight lines. "All right! All right. As long as Kimberly earns the theatergoers attention, then she is worth a decent wage. But not a farthing more."

"Agreed!" Jonathan had the look of a cat who had just lapped up some cream.

"But Jonathan, I—" Kimberly didn't like the thought of taking advantage of the others just because of her good luck. Besides, this meant that even more would be expected of her next time.

"Hush! It's done." There was a sparkle in his eye. "If you can help the players by giving our company a mystique, then you are well worth the extra pennies."

Indeed, Kimberly was inundated with letters and gifts from several admirers, including candy and flowers. Feeling like a little child at Christmas time, she sat in her room at the inn, opening up each and every paper-covered surprise.

"Merry-go-up!" There was even a note from the King himself, telling her that he wanted to meet her.

It was unbelievable. Only a few months ago she'd been toiling away at her uncle's tavern and now suddenly she was being gossiped about. Yet there were times when that fact troubled her. She didn't want to become too well known for fear that what happened at the inn might catch up with her and thereby with Christopher. Even with her dark wig, someone from the inn, who had traveled to London, might recognize her.

"Flowers for the lady Tremaine!" A young lad that Kimberly recognized as one of the "hawker's" sons entered the tent carrying an armful of bouquets.

"Soon I'll have so many flowers someone will think I want to become a flowerseller," Kimberly said with a sigh. She took it upon herself to relieve the boy of his burden, sniffing the blossoms appreciatively.

She then busied herself in finding glasses and tankards in which to put the various bunches of blooms. Red, pink, blue and yellow petals made her room as colorful as a field in spring. Someone, or several someones, had been very thoughtful and generous.

Kimberly was curious. Taking the note from one of the bouquets, she opened it up. "Christopher!" The name stung her eyes with tears. "It can't be." But the bouquet was from him. Every single flower.

"Miss?" The lad was surprised by her outburst. "Do you know the man?"

"Yes . . . !"

At first Kimberly suspected he had recognized her, but as she scanned the words he'd written, her anger flared. He was flirting with the mysterious actress, Velvet, not trying to renew their foolishly brief love affair. It seemed an all too strong reminder of his perfidy.

"He seeks to make another conquest." And break another woman's heart. The pompous rogue! Even the note reeked of arrogance. He wanted her to arrange a meeting at the inn, as if she were a common trollop anxious for his favors. Well, the devil take him! She would scorn him as he deserved. Perhaps it would do him some good to see that not every woman succumbed as easily as she once had!

"I want nothing to do with these flowers!" she told the startled flower boy.

In a voice tinged with anger, she instructed him to return the bouquet at once to the man who had purchased them.


Christopher was all decked out in his finest coat and breeches. He had even put lace at his throat, a surrender to fashion he seldom allowed himself. Tapping his foot impatiently, he waited, curious about the new actress. And yet why was he so concerned. She wasn't the first lovely woman to catch London's eye, nor would she be the last.

"Kimberly . . ."

Strange how *she* popped into his head when he least expected it. There were moments when he felt such regret, such remorse that he nearly became melancholy. But it was too late now. Hopefully she had forgotten all about him and was keeping company with some marriageable fellow. If so, he wished her well. She deserved happiness.

And what about him? He'd spent all of his free time studying his lines, practicing his walk, his sword fighting. He didn't want to be second best to any other actor. And so far he wasn't. Moreover his play had been welcomed with enthusiasm by the other actors, so much so that he was writing another. Why then wasn't he happy? Why wasn't his success in the theater enough?

Christopher squinted against the setting sun, looking toward the area where theaters were sprouting up like mushrooms. The theater was his life. His love of it had kept him going even during the days of Cromwell. Upon the stage he could be anyone that he chose. He could be old or young, loved or scorned, hero or villein. Yet, strangely enough there were times when he saw the image of a country cottage in his dreams.

"B'God!" He didn't like the way he was thinking. It would bode him no good.

"Sir!"

Turning around, Christopher was surprised to see the hawker's son. In his hand were a multitude of flowers.

"What is this!" Christopher's voice was a growl as he gestured the lad toward him.

The boy winced under Christopher's scrutiny. "She . . . she told me to return them. She does not want them."

"What?"

The lad seemed eager to please. "Perhaps . . . perhaps they make her sneeze."

"Didn't want them?" *What kind of woman didn't want flowers?* "Insufferable, ungrateful wench!"

"She said to tell you thank you," the boy recoiled as if afraid that he would be struck, "but she has no need for them."

"No need?" Christopher's pride burst like a bubble. "Perhaps you didn't make her understand who they were from?" After all, he was one of the most well-known men in his profession.

"She knew. She read your note."

He shook his head, not believing the boy's words at first. Then slowly it dawned on him. She was snubbing him. Why? Because they were in rival companies? Or was there another reason?

"And did she . . . did she tell you what I should do with them?"

The lad shook his head. "Aye. She said that you might bedeck the graves in the bone orchard."

"The graveyard!" It was like a slap in the face. Christopher gritted his teeth. "Alas, it seems my generosity has gone amiss."

"Sir . . . ?"

Christopher's anger knew no bounds. "Then take them there! Put them on the graves of all who died for the King." He'd meant his gesture as a show of friendship, but it was something akin to war to be so brutally rebuffed. It fired his frustration. At that moment he made a vow. If it was the last thing he did in this life, he would bring this haughty wench down.

# Twelve

It was to be war between the two acting companies, the one at Salisbury Court and the other at the Red Bull, egged on by Kimberly's and Christopher's pride, anger and determination for vengeance. Whatever one company did, the other would attempt to surpass. Whatever play one company decided to put on, the other would try to mount one that was more colorful, longer, more exciting. The sets got bigger and grander, the costumes brighter.

When Kimberly was given the lead in *The Taming of the Shrew* as Jonathan desired, playbills announced that Christopher Sheldon would head the cast of *All's Well That Ends Well*.

"Here's hoping that it does and that we do not come out the loser in this fight of yours," Richard Fletcher said to his friend as he handed out the lines. "And all because you were scorned by a woman."

Christopher scowled. "Not for that reason. I but want our company to make a name for itself and not be ignored." He was indignant. "Our actors are the more experienced ones. I would hate to see us left behind, all for the sake of some haughty little chit who takes herself much too seriously."

"Aha!" Richard tapped the paper he held in his hand. "Then you admit that you are prompted in part by revenge!"

"Revenge. Ha!" Christopher made a grab for his part of the script. "I have never even met this 'Velvet.'" He put a hand to his brow.

"Then perhaps it is time that you did." Richard folded his arms across his chest. "Or have you never heard of the Trojan Horse?"

Christopher thought long and hard. "I see. A change in strategy is what you are suggesting."

"It is."

Kimberly put on a blue satin robe and sat before the mirror, brushing her long blond hair so vigorously she nearly tore it out. She had heard from Christopher again. His note had said that he'd seen several of her performances and that he longed to meet her, for artistic reasons.

"Artistic reasons indeed." With a sarcastic laugh she picked up her dark wig, staring at it soulfully.

Christopher Sheldon was playing havoc with her life and her emotions. *Stay away from Christopher Sheldon, forget him!* It was much easier said than done. Certainly he had no intentions of letting her elude him, or so it seemed. And yet she *had* to. Succumbing to his charm would only bring heartache and possibly worse.

"How sad . . ."

She'd wanted Christopher's affection once, had dreamed about it night after night. Now that dream had turned sour, for she was caught in her own trap and wasn't quite sure what to do about it. She didn't dare reveal who she was, lest she put her very heart in danger. What then?

Kimberly was deep in thought as she dabbed at her rouge and powder. She thought of all the reasons she should hate Christopher. He was a man who was overly fond of women. That alone made any affection for him out of the question. He had left her, with only a money pouch as his goodbye, as if she were naught but some whore. He was heartless to have done such a thing. And now he was casually pursuing someone he hadn't even met. What better proof did she need that he was the worst kind of scoundrel?

"Christopher Sheldon wants to meet me only because I have piqued his curiosity, his sense of mystery," she whispered to her image in the mirror. "But I am much better off without him."

Closing her eyes Kimberly tried to forget him, but his face hovered in her mind's eye. The way his hair brushed his shoulders, the shape of his nose, the strength of his arms, the way he walked and talked—all haunted her. And his mouth . . . full and artfully chiseled, possessing a sensuous curve when he smiled. Touching her lips, she remembered his kiss and felt a warm glow flicker through her.

"No," she murmured. "I won't let him turn me into a love-sick ninny!"

*He left you alone. He won your heart and then he deserted you. How can you even think of seeing him again?* Her mind screamed a warning that was rejected by her heart. She tried to tell herself again and again that Christopher Sheldon was a cruel, unfeeling man, yet how could she forget the gentleness he had displayed when they had made love? There had been concern in his eyes when her uncle had scolded her. And he had fought for her honor. How could she forget?

She was still in love with him, Kimberly decided, a fact which made her all the more adamant in her determination not to succumb to his charms again, no matter how hard he pursued her.

She began to dress, hanging her robe on a peg by the door. Slipping on her chemise and petticoats, she padded across the floor on bare feet to the table. She poured water into the basin to wash her face and hands, and picking up her worn hairbrush, she began to brush her luxuriant waves until her hair crackled.

Kimberly was tired. Her arms ached with tension. Today had been strenuous. And yet it was worth it, wasn't it? Certainly her fame was spreading, more quickly than she ever might have imagined. She was pleased, Jonathan was happy and the other actors were ecstatic. Why then did she have such an empty feeling inside?

Sitting down in front of the large mirror that acted as her vanity, she studied herself in the glass. She ought to be happy, and yet she wasn't. The problem was, she knew why.

"Oh, Christopher . . . !" Putting her elbows on the vanity, she rested her forehead on her hands.

At first Christopher was certain he had entered the wrong room, for the young woman who occupied this tiny chamber had long, glossy blond hair not brown. One glance at the dark wig, however, changed his mind. So the mysterious Velvet was not a brunette after all. Just in case, however, he called out her name.

His voice was much louder than he had intended, causing the woman to jump.

"What are you doing in here?" she demanded in a trembling whisper without turning around. In protection of her modesty, she grabbed the blue robe, adjusting the neckline.

He shrugged his shoulders, not showing the least bit of remorse for having barged right in. "I've come to see Velvet Tremaine. I assume that is *you.*"

"Then you assume right! I am *she!*"

Christopher took a step closer. Glancing in the mirror to get a good look at her face, he found himself looking into eyes as deep as the sea. Eyes he remembered. No, it couldn't be. He was seeing things. He passed a hand in front of his eyes, but the vision of loveliness did not fade away. His voice was choked as he whispered her name soundlessly. "Kimberly!"

At hearing him speak her name, Kimberly gasped. Her eyes met his in the mirror, and she knew that she was lost. There could be no denying who she was. "Yes!" A hodgepodge of emotions swept over her at seeing Christopher Sheldon. Though she had been expecting their paths to cross someday she still wasn't prepared for the storm of feelings he unleashed. Her masquerade was over.

"Kimberly Bowen!" But then, perhaps he wasn't all that surprised. Perhaps somewhere deep in his heart he had suspected it.

"Why did you come?" Her expression grew hard, her soft mouth tightened. She tried to keep the quiver out of her voice by being overly stern.

"Why?" He shook his head. "Forsooth, I do not really know." Somehow he regained his composure. "I thought you would return to Reedham, marry some rich swain and have a baby year after year. Why the theater?"

"A woman does what she must to survive," she said dryly.

Standing there with her eyes flashing, she was the loveliest vision he had ever seen. Her beauty had blossomed. His eyes drank in the sight of her, as he remembered how she'd felt in his arms. The smell of her. The taste of her.

"Kim . . . !" He towered above her.

"It's Velvet now!" she snapped. "Kimberly Bowen is dead. She died the night you so callously left her."

"I can explain . . ." He hung his head. Could he? Would mere words atone for what he had done? "Kimberly . . ."

Seeing her again was like being dealt a physical blow. Christopher's heart constricted in his chest painfully each time she glanced his way. He had been a fool to leave her. Now it was too late to make amends. He knew she would never forgive him. Even so, he couldn't leave it like this. He wanted her back.

"Kimberly, we were happy traveling side by side. And believe it or not, when I made love to you, that was the most wonderful night of my life." He took a deep breath, letting it out in a sigh. "We could be lovers again. . . ."

"No!" Christopher Sheldon was not the marrying kind, but she was. "I will never be a man's lover." When she gave herself to a man again it would be in the marriage bed. No more would she put herself in a position where a man could just up and leave her.

"Kimberly. . . ." His voice was husky and seductive. Bending down, he kissed the hollow of her neck.

Her flesh tingled. Damn him! Damn herself. How could she be so weak as to desire to capitulate to this gesture. She wanted him to take her in his arms, carry her to her bed and make love to her. It was her deepest longing. That was why she pulled away so violently, snapping, "Leave me be!"

"You don't mean that."

"I do!" Hastily she sought for something to say that would keep him at bay. "I'm . . . I'm in love with someone else." She stiffened at hearing the lie.

"What?" He hadn't been prepared for this. It seemed an invisible fist had hit him in the stomach. "Who?" he asked sarcastically, "another actor, I suppose." Who else could it be? Hopefully not the King.

"Jonathan Fairfax." She dug her fingernails into her palms to keep from crying aloud.

"Jonathan!" He swore aloud. "That fool of an actor doesn't know the first thing about being upon the stage."

She hurried to defend her friend. "He does. He taught me everything that I know."

"How kind of him!" His jealousy showed. The thought of any other man touching her, now that he had seen her again, was just too disturbing. Reaching out, he put his hand on her arm in a gesture he meant to be apologetic. "Kimberly, I was wrong. Can't you ever forgive me . . . ?"

She turned on him. "No! Never. I trusted you, loved you, and you threw me away without even a backward glance. I never want to see you again." Her expression was so fierce he knew she meant it.

"Well, I want to see you, and I will! I never give up what's mine, 'Velvet,' " he said sarcastically. "Just remember that."

As silently and suddenly as he had come, he was gone.


The rivalry between Michael Mohun's company at the Red Bull and William Beeston's at Salisbury Court had taken a dangerous turn. Having resumed the position of Master of Revels, which he had held under Charles I, Sir Henry Herbert had licensed three acting companies, one at the Cockpit, one at

Salisbury and one at the Bull. Now the rivalry had spread to other companies anxious to take advantage of London's fascination with the theater.

Unknowing of this, the King had meanwhile awarded a monopoly on theatrical production in London to William Davenant and Thomas Killigrew, who had grown up at the English court and been with the royal family throughout its exile. The King's Company it was called. The claim had been put forth that it had in its midst the older and more experienced actors of England.

"Aye, older!" Jonathan said with scorn. "All of them long in the beard."

Certainly the fact that they were in the king's favor put a whole new light on the matter. Technically all four companies were legitimate, despite outcries to the contrary. Still, it made the matter of performances all the more competitive.

Kimberly's company could take little time to savor their triumphs. Always at the backs of the actors' minds was the thought that in order to survive they had to be grander and better than any other company. Kimberly had twice as many lines to learn and more pressure put upon her to do well.

During the day she had numerous things to think about and thereby was able to put Christopher from her mind. At night, however, he haunted her dreams.

How could he! Kimberly's bottom lip trembled as she thought of the arrogance Christopher had displayed. And yet she couldn't put from her mind the gentle touch of his hands, the way he had caressed her once. His fingers had brought forth fire wherever they'd moved, causing her body to ache with suppressed passion even at the memory.

Night after night she tossed and turned, remembering. She was assailed by a feeling of bitter disappointment that she had not let him make love to her. Instead, they had argued.

"Juliet is a part made just for her. She would be the perfect actress to play to my Romeo. Don't you agree?"

Staring at the candles used to illuminate the stage, Kimberly hurriedly brought herself back to the present.

"The part is suitable in every way for you, Velvet." He nudged her in the ribs. "A woman who thinks love is worth dying for." He cocked his head. "Would you die for love of a man? Would you die for me?"

She shook her head. "No."

He sighed. "Ah, well . . ."

"Men and women who die for the sake of love are figments of a writer's imagination." Life was fact not fantasy. Clenching her teeth she looked at Jonathan. He was kind, steadfast and true. What's more, he always thought about what was in her best interest. Why then did the thought of Jonathan holding her in his arms leave her cold?

Christopher fidgeted as he sat at the inn's large table. He drummed his fingers nervously and tapped the toe of his boot against the floor. Usually calm and composed, he was a bundle of nerves as he remembered what Kimberly Bowen had told him.

"Jonathan Fairfax." It didn't make sense. The man was so dull, so boring. He was not the kind of man to win the heart of a beautiful woman. That is, unless it was a case of gratitude.

"She loves me! No matter what she says. I know it." He was stunned, disappointed. Still he knew he could never forget her, decidedly not now. "You must win her back, Christopher. If you don't you will soon be bait for Bedlam!"

"What will you have, sir?" asked a shrill voice, startling him out of his misery.

"Ale. Dark," he answered, looking up to find himself the object of severe scrutiny. Trying to sooth his injured pride and test his charms, he boldly winked, though the buxom miss was clearly not his type.

"Anything else?" She leaned over, affording him a look at the enormous breasts which threatened to pop from her bodice. The gleam in her eye offered an invitation.

He ought to take her up on what she offered, he thought with a glower, yet just the thought of pursuing anyone but

Kimberly was a troubling one. As he eyed this woman up and down, he compared her ample curves to Kimberly's delicately shaped breasts, so soft and alluring, and any passion he might have felt quickly cooled. God's blood, she had ruined him for any other woman.

"Just the ale!" he exclaimed, making his lack of interest plain. The tavern maid stalked away in silence, casting him a sullen look when at last she brought his mug. Taking a long drink, Christopher had a notion to drown his sorrows. He was totally consumed with his misery, helpless to stop the pain that even thinking of Kimberly in Jonathan Fairfax's arms brought forth.

"How can she think seriously of Jonathan?" he muttered, choking on the very thought. Not that there was anything really wrong with the other man, except that he was dull.

Jealousy. He had never experienced the emotion before, and he didn't like it. The image of Kimberly lying in his arms came back to him, her golden hair spread about her slim body like a living cloak of gold. She had been all loving softness. How could he ever forget that night in the stables? Their passion had been as shattering as an earthquake, a storm. How could he ever forget how wonderful their lovemaking had been?

He couldn't, and he wouldn't.

Practically flying out the door he hurried to the stables, saddled one of the company's horses and was off.

# Thirteen

The fire in the great hearth leaped and sparked, warding off the chill of the night. By the light of the lamp, Kimberly studied her pages of the script, wishing with all her heart that she had even half the spunk of Katherina. And yet even Katherina had been tamed. Perhaps then, when all was said and done, it really was a man's world.

It was quiet in the inn. Most of the other patrons were abed, and that was why she was so startled by the loud tapping at her door. Surely Christopher wouldn't have the fortitude to return. Not after what she had told him. Glancing at the mantel clock, she saw that the hour was nine.

Kimberly waited for just a moment, but when the insistent knocking began again she slowly moved to the door. To her surprise she found Christopher standing there, leaning against the doorframe. The faint hint of ale teased her nostrils as he stepped closer.

"Christopher, I have nothing more to say to you! Nothing at all."

"Well I have something to say." His voice was different, as was his face, though he smiled.

She tried to close the door, but his foot acted as a doorstop. There was a reckless glitter in the eyes staring back at her. His hair fell forward across his forehead and into his eyes. Usually well groomed, he looked slightly disheveled, his shirt open down the front and revealing the strength of his neck and a tuft of hair on his chest.

"Oh no. If you think—"

He pushed past her with a predatory grace. Slowly his eyes moved over her as he shut the door behind them. Walking toward her, he reached out and touched the hair falling over her temples, then closed his fingers in a fist. She was so very lovely. He had been the world's biggest fool to leave her.

"I came to tell you that I love you!" His eyes strayed over her, lingering with grim appreciation on the slim column of her neck and the full, tempting line of her breasts. He remembered the heat and warmth of her skin, the taste of her, her softness; and an intense, nearly painful surge of desire swept through him, tempered with a much gentler feeling.

"Love . . . ?" She wanted to believe. Still, there was so much bitterness inside her. "Methink you do not know the meaning of the word."

"I do now!"

"Love," she said again. How was it possible her world could so suddenly be crumbling around her? She had reorganized her life. Why had he turned it into a shambles?

"Let me prove it to you. I want to start all over again. . . ." His hands closed around her shoulders, and she was jerked unceremoniously up against the hardness of his chest as his mouth descended, taking hers with a savage intensity. He kissed her like a man with a fierce, insatiable hunger to appease. The touch of his mouth evoked just such a hunger in her. Love was a healing thing. Perhaps she should give him a chance.

Reaching up, she wound her arms around his neck, kissing him back.

His lips were everywhere—her cheeks, her earlobes, her neck and back to her mouth again, his tongue plunging deeply, insistently between her lips. Her hands moved restlessly over his chest, then up to become entangled in his long, dark hair. His hands answered her caress, sliding down her body. Then he was sweeping her up in his arms and carrying her toward the stairs.

Moonlight streamed through the open curtains, casting eerie shadows on the wall as Christopher made his way to the bed with his beautiful bundle. His mouth was hungry as it took hers, plundering, moving urgently as he explored her mouth's sweetness. The pressure of the kiss should have hurt her, but it didn't. Instead it drained her of her very soul, then poured it back in again, filling her to overflowing. Despite her anger, that kiss proved to her that he cared. It was not lust alone that fueled him, no matter what she might have thought in the past.

So thinking, she returned his kiss, her defenses demolished by the cravings of her own body. There was nothing in the world for her but his mouth. She surrendered to him completely without even a token resistance, wishing the kiss could go on forever. Twining her hands around his neck she clutched him to her, eagerly pressing her body against his chest. She could feel the heat and strength and growing desire of him. She loved him, and he wanted her. For the moment she was content.

Christopher pulled his mouth away, looking deep into her eyes. He read passion there and trust. A trust he vowed never to betray.

With that thought in mind, he deposited her on the huge bed and lowered himself down beside her. As he reached for her, she found herself imprisoned on the feather mattress. She heard the soft rhythm of his breathing as he spread her golden hair in a cloak about her shoulders.

"I like you much better with golden hair. You are beautiful. So bloody lovely."

With questing fingers he unfastened her gown and pulled the material away from her shoulders. She could feel his hands forcing her gown lower, felt the warmth of his fingers as they touched and caressed. She couldn't bring herself to utter a protest, even when he touched the peaks of her breasts.

"Tell me that you don't love Jonathan. Tell me that you still love me."

She didn't lie. "I love you still, Christopher. I always have, believe that or not." Kimberly moaned as his palm cupped her sensitive breast, and that sound took away all his resolve. "I do love you!"

Closing her eyes, she refused to think of anything that might bring her back to reality. He was the man she loved. Her body had recognized that from the first moment she had laid eyes on him. Christopher, her Christopher. She had spent so many nights dreaming that he would make love to her, she wouldn't let anger spoil it now.

"Christopher . . ." His name was husky as she spoke it against his mouth. As his hands outlined the swells of her breasts, she sank into the softness of the feather mattress.

"So much wasted time," he murmured. "But now I'll make up for it." His head was bent low, his tongue curling around the tips of the breast he was about to suck gently. She responded with a breathless murmur, and her body flamed with desire. She ached to be naked against him. Did that make her a wanton? Then so be it.

Christopher breathed deeply, savoring the violet scent of her perfume. The enticing fragrance invaded his flaring nostrils, engulfing him.

"Kimberly . . ." Her name was a prayer on his lips.

Raising himself up on an elbow, he looked down at her, and at that moment he knew he'd put his heart and soul in pawn. Removing his shirt, he pressed their naked chests together, shivering at the sensation. It was vibrantly arousing, sending a flash of quicksilver through his veins.

It was hot in the room despite the chill in the air. Slowly, leisurely, Christopher stripped Kimberly's garments away as if he were removing the petals of a flower. His fingers lingered as they wandered down her stomach to explore the texture of her skin. Like velvet. He sought the indentation of her navel, then moved lower to tangle his fingers in the soft wisps of hair at the joining of her legs. Moving back a bit, he let his eyes enjoy what his hands had set free.

"Do you have any idea how much I want you? Do you?" he breathed out. Then he laughed. "Of course you do. That's the point in being so beautiful, isn't it? To tempt men beyond endurance. Well, you've won."

Swearing softly, he took her hand and pressed it to the firm flesh of his arousal. She felt the throbbing strength of him as her eyes gazed into his. Then he bent to kiss her, his mouth keeping hers a willing captive for a long, long time.

The warmth and heat of his lips, the memory of her fingers touching that private part of him, sent a sweet ache flaring through Kimberly. Growing bold she allowed her hands to explore, to delight in touching the firm flesh that covered his ribs, those broad shoulders, the muscles of his arms, the lean length of his back. He was so perfectly formed. Beautiful for a man. With a soft sigh, she curled her fingers in the thick, springy hair that furred his chest. Her fingers lightly circled in imitation of what he was doing to her.

Feeling encumbered by his clothes, Christopher pulled them off and flung them aside. Their bodies touched now in an intimate embrace, and yet he took his time, lost in this world of sensual delight. She was in his arms and in his bed. It was where she belonged. She was his, he would never let her go. Not now.

"Kimberly! Kimberly!"

They lay together, kissing, touching, rolling over and over on the soft bed. His hands were doing wondrous things to her, making her writhe and groan. Every inch of her body caught fire as passion exploded between them. He moved against her, sending waves of pleasure along every nerve in her body. The swollen length of him brushed across her thighs. Then he was covering her, his manhood probing at the entrance to her secret core.

"A long awaited pleasure," he whispered in her ear.

His kiss stopped any further words she might have uttered.

Tightening her thighs around his waist, Kimberly arched up to him with sensual urgency. She was melting inside, merging with him into one being. His lovemaking was like nothing she could ever have imagined, filling her, flooding her. Clinging to him, she called out his name.

Christopher groaned as her warm flesh sheathed the long length of him. He possessed her again and again. He didn't want it to end, didn't want suspicion to intrude into this warm wonderful haven they had all too briefly created.

# *Fourteen*

It was dark in the room and suffocatingly quiet. They did not speak, for neither really knew what to say. They had been swept away on a tide of longing that neither could deny. Where were they to go from here?

He desires me, but that's not the same as love. Does he really love me as he says? "Love," a word so often spoken but so rarely proven. It was not just the heated passion they had given in to that night. It was like what happened in the plays. It was listening to someone, caring about them, sharing your world, being there when they needed you. She was afraid to trust, afraid to take a chance.

Physically and emotionally drained, much too vulnerable now to face him with questions, she took refuge in the darkness and contented herself with listening to the pleasant sound of his low raspy breathing and with remembering. A deep yearning rose in her, a hope that it was not too late for happiness.

Oh, yes, his lovemaking had deeply affected her. Clasping her arms around her, she remembered every touch, every kiss and caress. Their being together had been the most beautiful moment of her life. It was as if she had been starving and only Christopher could whet her appetite. She wanted to be with him forever, to walk beside him, share in his dreams. But would he be there when she turned her head, or would he desert her once again?

Lying there and watching him, she was as still as stone. How did he feel about her? Did he love her, or had it been only his body's cravings that he had assuaged? When he had entered her she had felt her heart move, had been full of him, full of her love. The richest woman in the world. But what of Christopher? What was he dreaming about? Her?

Christopher's thoughts were as potent as Kimberly's. He closed his eyes, remembering. Never had he realized that passion could be like this, such shattering ecstasy as to be almost pain. Did he love her? Yes, if love was a mindless delight of the senses and the heart. And yet what to do about it?

Once again the vine-covered cottage floated in front of his eyes. The perfect dream for some. But would he really be happy if he settled down? Or would he feel caged, longing one day to break free? Could he give up the theater? Did he in fact need to? Kimberly now had her own career on the stage. Would that be enough for her? Most women wanted children. Did he? Did he want little replicas of himself playing hide-and-seek among the set pieces?

He sprawled in his chair, stretching his long legs out in front of him as he thought things out. But what was life without her? He had been miserable these past few months. He had felt that a part of him was missing. Last night he had felt whole.

Christopher was dressed only in his breeches. No shirt, no shoes. The thought kept tugging at his brain: he could so easily divest himself of his trousers and crawl into bed with her again. At this moment that was what he really wanted, and yet he held himself back.

"Bloody damn! Bloody damn!" he swore. He put his foot up on a low chest at the foot of the bed. Why couldn't things be simple? If what he felt was love as he firmly believed, then why didn't it make things easier and not harder?

"Kimberly, are you awake?" There was an edge to his voice that he tried to temper. A frustration with himself.

"Yes. I never went to sleep. I couldn't." She suddenly had

a need to talk, to make him understand. "You'll never know how helpless I felt when you left me, and yet when I went to the theater to see you in *Hamlet,* a part of me understood. You're like a bird, Christopher. You have to fly. You would never survive if you had your wings clipped."

"Sssshhh. I really don't want to talk about it now." It took every ounce of resolve he had not to go to her and take her in his arms.

He didn't, but she did. "My mother once tried to make me understand about my father. He had loved her, he had loved us both, she said, but he went away. She waited so patiently, so lovingly for his return. He never did come back." She clenched her fists. "There were times when I hated him for that. He had wounded her so deeply. Now I remember that she said, if you love something, set it free. If it comes back to you, it is yours. If it doesn't, it never belonged to you in the first place."

"She sounds like a very wise woman." There was a long pause. "I will never leave you again, Kim. I want you to believe that."

"A part of me does . . ."

"I need to do some thinking, Kimberly. Some deep, serious thinking. Until I do, I don't want to say anything or make any commitments. Please understand."

"Christopher . . ." She loved him, there was no doubt of that. Her senses were filled with wanting him. Then go to him, a voice inside her head whispered. Life was all too short, so uncertain. One never knew what the future held in store. But he was here with her now, and she wanted him to make love to her again. If he couldn't make any promises, well, so be it.

Rising from the bed, Kimberly padded across the hard wooden floor on bare feet. Leaning toward him she stroked his neck, tangling her fingers in his hair. Christopher closed his eyes, giving himself up to the rippling pleasure.

"Make love to me again . . ." She leaned forward to brush his mouth with her lips. That simple gesture said all she wanted to say, that she loved him, that she desired him. Slowly his hands closed around her shoulders, pulling her to him, and he answered her shy kiss with a passion that made her gasp. Gathering her into his arms, he then carried her back to the bed.

"I do love you, so very much." His hands roamed gently over her body, lingering on the fullness of her ripe breasts, leaving no part of her free of his touch.

She gave herself up to the fierce emotions that raced through her, answering his touch with searching hands, returning his caresses. Wrapping her arms around his neck, she offered herself to him, writhing against him in a slow delicate dance. She could feel the pulsating hardness of him through the fabric of his trousers, and reached up to pull his breeches from him. If that was being overbold and brazen she didn't care.

Sweet hot desire fused their bodies together as he leaned against her. His strength mingled with her softness, his hands moving up her sides, warming her with his heat. Like a fire his lips burned a path from one breast to the other, bringing forth spirals of pulsating sensation that swept over her like a storm.

Christopher's mouth fused with hers, his kiss deepening as his touch grew bolder. Kimberly luxuriated in the pleasure of his lovemaking, stroking him and kissing him back. He slid his hands between their bodies, poised above her. The tip of his maleness pressed against her; then he entered her softness in a slow but strong thrust, joining her in that most intimate of embraces. He kissed her as their naked bodies fused, and from the depths of her soul, her heart cried out.

Christopher filled her with his love, leaving her breathless. No applause, no platitudes, no amount of fame could compete with what she felt now. Her arms locked around him as she arched to meet his body in a sensuous dance, forgetting all her inhibitions as she expressed her love. Then a warm explosion burst through her.

Even when the sensual magic was over they clung to each other. Smiling, she lay curled in the crook of Christopher's arm, and he, his passion spent, lay close to her, his body pressing against hers. They were together. It was all she had for now. For the moment it had to be enough.

Long after Christopher had left, Kimberly sat by the window, staring out at the horizon. For all her talk of freedom she knew in her heart that they belonged together. If only he would see. Still, she would never tie him down. Love had to come from the heart and not from any other kind of tie.

The sun had come up. Its bright light made it hot in the room. Kimberly threw open the shutters, but it was still uncomfortable. Feeling closed in, needing a breath of fresh air, she hurried to dress, then opened the door to her room and tiptoed down the stairs.

Outside the air was sweet with the smell of flowers. Birds trilled. The world was a beautiful place. Strange, she thought, how a leisurely stroll could bring such a feeling of calm. The sights, smells and sounds brought a peacefulness to her soul as she sorted out her thoughts and feelings.

She heard a twig snap. Looking around, she somehow expected to see Christopher. Instead another face greeted her. One just as familiar. Reaching out he grabbed her by the wrist.

"Jonathan . . . ?"

"Velvet! Velvet! Velvet!" He pulled her toward him until they were nose to nose. "Or should I say Kimberly?"

There was a strange glitter in his eyes. She had never seen Jonathan like this. It made her wary. "Velvet will do. That *is* who I am."

He let her go, clenching his hands into fists. "I know who *you* are, but who was *he?*"

"Who?"

"The man who left your room at the inn." He shrugged. "Forsooth, there is no reason to hide the fact that I was spying. I always keep an eye on you. 'Tis my habit."

She felt an obligation to Jonathan to be truthful. He deserved better than to be the brunt of a game. "That was Christopher Sheldon."

"Sheldon!" Of course he knew the name. "Why that bastard! Come no doubt to try and sweep you away." His eyes narrowed into slits. "What did he offer you to move on to the other acting company?"

"He didn't—"

This time he grabbed both her arms with a grip that hurt her. "You belong to me, Velvet Tremaine. I found you. I molded you."

Kimberly pulled away. "I don't belong to anyone, except to myself!" She was grateful to him; indeed, he was perhaps her dearest friend, but that did not give him any kind of claim on her.

His expression went from anger to a look of fear. "I . . . I know. I know. I only meant . . ." His eyes swept over her with a hunger that made her cheeks burn, as if he knew what she looked like unclothed. "I don't want to lose you, Velvet. Nor do the others."

"You won't." Taking a step back, she hurriedly reassured him. "I am perfectly happy with the players. I would never think to be unloyal. Besides, that is not what Christopher Sheldon came to see me about."

"Then what . . . ?" He looked suspicious.

"Jonathan . . . ?"

It must have been the expression in her eyes that gave her away. "He's your lover. That's it, isn't it? B'God, that arrogant, two-shilling actor has slipped between your legs."

She flushed to the roots of her hair. It was true, yet Jonathan didn't know the true history of her relationship with his rival. "You don't understand! I . . . I knew Christopher long before I met you. He . . . he left me outside of London just before your horse came riding by."

"How gallant of him," Jonathan said mockingly.

Kimberly hastened to defend her lover. "Who among us has

not made mistakes? The important thing is, he has tried to set things right between us."

"Set things right?" The muscles in his face twitched as he sorted it all out. "He loved you, left you and now has come thundering to your side like one of Shakespeare's heroes. Now that you are no ignorant country girl but a woman of reknown, he thinks to claim you again. Well, to hell with him, I say!"

"I love him, Jonathan. From the first moment I looked into his eyes."

"Love." The way he said it made it sound like a curse.

"Aye, love," she pleaded softly. "Please understand."

"No!" Jonathan was adamant. "I can't! I won't!" He mumbled on and on as if giving a soliloquy, as if for a moment he had forgotten she was even there. "He was a bastard to her. Seduced her then up and left. I took her in. I showed her every consideration. I was a gentleman. In gratitude, she chases after him at the first crook of his little finger."

"No, it wasn't like that. I was hurt, angry." Just as Jonathan was now. Oh, how could she have been so blind to his feelings for her? How could she have hurt him? "Jonathan, you have been very good to me, and I'll never forget that but—"

"I know what he did. I know all about Reedham and your uncle." The muscles along his jaw quivered, his expression became hard. Bitter.

"What?" She hadn't been prepared for this. For just a moment she felt the world was spinning.

"He cold-bloodedly struck your uncle down! He, an expert swordsman."

She paled, her heart pounding all the while. "It was a matter of self-defense. He didn't want to, didn't mean to."

"Self-defense." He laughed and said smugly, "Of course you would say that it was, but then what might the townsmen say?"

"The townsmen?" The truth dawned on her. Someone had come to London from Reedham and recognized her despite her dark-haired wig. That same someone had started snooping and had thereby recognized Christopher as well. But how had Jonathan found out all of this? "You have not been told the truth, Jonathan. My uncle was miserly and cruel. Christopher was but taking up for me. My uncle, in his cups, reached for a sword and instigated the kind of fight for which he had no skills. He forced Christopher to fight him. The fatal blow, however, was an accident. I know. I was there."

"So . . . ?" It was then that Jonathan revealed the ruthless side of his nature. He offered her an ultimatum. If she left with Christopher Sheldon, or even tried to see him again, he vowed angrily that he would betray the handsome actor to the King's men.

"You wouldn't!" But looking at his face, she knew he would.

# *Fifteen*

Christopher awoke, bone tired and yet at peace with himself. He had unburdened his conscience. He had declared his love. For the first time in a long while he really did feel that he had begun a whole new life. A life in which instead of applause, speeches and bows, the woman he truly cared for was at the center. At the moment there was only room for Kimberly in his heart and soul.

He lay on his back with his eyes closed, luxuriating in the sun streaming through his window at the inn, rays of warmth dancing across his naked body. Weeks of frustration just seemed to melt away. She was his! At last she had granted him the glorious sweetness of her body again. But had she given him her forgiveness? If not, then he would make certain that she did. This morning it seemed that anything was possible.

Heaven. Her body had been pure heaven. Kimberly had made him the happiest man alive! He smiled as he thought of her responses to him last night. It gave him a heady feeling of power to have been able to bring her such deep satisfaction. Not once but several times. He remembered her muffled noises of pleasure as she tried to stifle her moans with the back of her hand, and he instinctively reached out for the image of Kimberly that danced before his eyes. Just the memory of her long legs, her breasts, the tantalizing way she had wound her legs around him, and had arched up to meet his thrusts brought a certain part of him very much alive.

"Steady . . . steady. . . ." Taking a deep breath Christopher forced himself to cool down. "All in good time . . ." Running his fingers through his long, dark hair, he sat up chuckling. "Right after I have had breakfast!"

Christopher put his bare feet on the cold wooden floor one at a time, bending to retrieve his garments. His gray breeches, white shirt, stockings, boots and jacket were scattered on the floor in a haphazard manner, proof of just how tired he had been when he'd come back to his room early this morning. He had wanted to stay with her, but fearing for her reputation he had regretfully left. But there would come a time when he would never have to do that.

" 'My love's more ponderous than my tongue, . . .' " he said aloud, quoting *King Lear*. Indeed, every speech he had given concerning love now rang in his ears.

Even during the performance of *All's Well That Ends Well*, later that day he thought of her, and it was as if he were hearing Shakespeare's words through different ears. As he watched and listened, waiting for his cues, he became absorbed in the flow of words. Love did "make the world go 'round."

Christopher's eyes left the actors for just a moment as he scanned the crowd. How many people were sitting in the galleries, standing on the ground? More than a thousand, he guessed. An odd gathering. People who would never rub elbows ordinarily. And yet, in one thing they were all the same. Each and every one of them was, in one way or another, looking for love, or at least what they thought it to be.

Suddenly the blood drained from Christopher's face. His fingers tingled, his heart froze in his chest. He forgot all about the play, the audience and where he was as his gaze focused on a man he recognized all too well. It couldn't be. And yet it was. He would never forget that face! Nor did it seem the man had forgotten his, for upon realization that he had been seen, he fled from the crowd.

"Harold Bowen!!" No, it wasn't possible. Ghosts didn't really exist. And yet, whoever it was looked just like him; there could be no mistake. "Wait!" The word passed through Christopher's lips before he could think. Then years of experience took hold. Deftly he leaped off the stage, heading for the man he thought he had killed.

Christopher kept his quarry in his sights as he pushed and shoved his way through the crowd, who, thinking his actions to be part of the play, did little to assist him. Fascinated by the proceedings, they formed a human wall that stood between Christopher and the man whose identity he now had to know.

"Come back!" Quickly Christopher pushed through a small opening, hoping to corner Kimberly's uncle before the man got away. At the very least, the man owed him an explanation.

"Who's he after? What's going on?" Excitement ruled the crowd, while they stared, eyes and mouths agog, as Christopher moved stealthfully away.

But Harold Bowen was fleet of foot, despite his age. Pushing and ducking, he quickly put Christopher at a distance as he fought desperately to escape. Christopher had never moved so fast in his life! He ran until his lungs threatened to burst. Even so, the surly innkeeper managed to stay just out of his reach.

"B'God! He's a speedy weasel!" Christopher gasped as he headed out toward the cobbled street.

He might have caught up with his quarry, had it not been for a rickety hay wagon rumbling out from an alleyway. It delayed him just long enough for Harold Bowen to get a head start again. Christopher was exasperated as he lost sight of Kimberly's uncle. Still, what had happened had eased his mind. Either Harold Bowen had a twin or he was alive. But what was he doing in London? The answer seemed obvious. No doubt he had come in search of his niece. But that man would never get Kimberly in his clutches again. That was a vow Christopher made over and over as he returned to the inn. There he found the actors gathered together at the table, eating, drinking and enjoying their favorite pastime of all, talking.

"Christopher, you had best hurry and take your share while

there is still food aplenty." Richard Fletcher smiled. "We're celebrating." He wiped his mouth with the hem of the table-cloth.

Christopher was famished. He didn't need any prodding to unleash his appetite. Plopping down on a chair next to the playwright he relished the dishes set before him, expecting severe rebuke for what he had done earlier. Instead Richard made light of Christopher's actions.

"I like the change you made to the play, Christopher. If Shakespeare were still alive I would wager that he would approve, too. It made the audience feel they were part of the action," he said. "So much so that we just might keep it in." He laughed.


Summer storm clouds and sunlight competed for control of the afternoon. As Kimberly looked toward the sky she thought the weather matched her own confusion and turmoil. Flee or fight? Cry or shout? Give up or give in? Jonathan had her trapped; he knew her darkest fears. What was she going to do?

Of a certainty she had spent a sleepless night, going over in her mind the argument she'd had with Jonathan. How could she have so thoroughly misjudged the man? Kind? Gentle? Caring? Not the man who had threatened to send Christopher to Newgate for something he knew to be a matter of self-defense, an accident. He was selfish, scheming, manipulative, she could see that now. He had had a motive when he'd taken her under his wing.

"Oh, Christopher . . . !" Just when the world had promised her rainbows Jonathan's scheming threatened to spoil everything. It was like some ghastly play, ill written at best. But what if they ran away?

To go where? London was the center of the theater in England. To France? To Italy? No, they would never be happy out of England.

Kimberly was tense, confused and deeply troubled. She had

thought her days at the inn were behind her, but they had risen up to haunt her. And to haunt Christopher.

The next few days were painful, for though Kimberly longed with all her heart to be with Christopher, she had to avoid him at all costs. She couldn't take a chance that Jonathan, in a fit of jealousy, might do something that would endanger her lover's freedom. And yet, how could she let Jonathan win? How could she allow him to hold a hatchet over Christopher's head for the rest of their lives?

Kimberly felt like a caged bird, trapped. And yet the alternative, seeing Christopher rolled off in the cart to prison, or worse yet to Tyburn tree, was even more disquieting. With a shudder, she remembered seeing the hanging of the highwayman called Scar several years ago. It had been gruesome.

Indeed, the next few days seemed endless, and she hadn't a moment's peace of mind. It was becoming harder and harder to avoid Christopher. Only by staying at the theater until the wee hours of the night, or hiding in the tiring-room, had she been able to escape him. She had even taken to sleeping at the theater, fearful lest Christopher pay a visit to her room.

At night, alone and aching to be in his arms, she succumbed to her dreams, frightening nightmares that left her trembling when she awoke. In these dreams she was watching the proceedings in the court room at the Old Bailey. As at the theater, people were noisy, laughing, but this macabre crowd was jeering Christopher, not applauding him, as he was brought in. Jostling each other, they fought for seats that would give them a good view of the proceedings.

"There he is, Christopher Sheldon. How low he has been brought, and all for the sake of a woman." Kimberly stood wearily with ten other unfortunates, barely aware of what was going on.

The judge and counsel in their intricately curled white wigs blended into the blur of the crowd, scowling as Christopher walked by. In the dream Kimberly tried to run to him, to beg the court's mercy, to tell them what had really happened. Instead she was forced to sit and watch a ghastly mummery.

It was a mockery from start to finish. All the patrons of her uncle's tavern were seated against the wall, smiles upon their flushed and bloated faces. One by one they gave their perjured testimonies. Christopher would have no justice here.

Again she tried, in her dream, to step forward, to tell the truth about what had occurred. Again she was detained, to watch helplessly as Jonathan stepped forward, speaking with the cunning elegance he always displayed on stage. Painting a verbal portrait, he wove a tangled web of lies that left no other verdict possible.

"Guilty," the judge declared.

"No! No!" Tossing and turning on the tiring room's couch Kimberly fought the arms that held her back, but there was nothing she could do. In the end she could only watch as Christopher was escorted from the room, through the heavy iron-studded door, then past the cells of Newgate.

Christopher's patience was wearing thin. A week, that was how long it had been since he had made love to Kimberly at the inn. He had thought it to be a new beginning, but suddenly she was avoiding him as if he had the pox. She was, in fact, acting as strangely as an inmate of Bedlam.

"It's lonely in my damned big bed." He wanted her beside him. Where she belonged. He thought she had decided that too, but maybe she needed more convincing.

The moon was just making its downward descent as he left her room at the inn. She hadn't come back. That seemed to be a pattern of late.

"God's Blood!" Jealousy took hold of him as Jonathan Fairfax came to mind. No, it couldn't be. Even so, Christopher's feet headed in the direction of Salisbury Court as if they had a will all their own.

# *Sixteen*

Someone was shaking her awake. Kimberly gasped. Opening her eyes wide, she struggled against her assailant. "Take your hands off me!" As her vision cleared she saw to her surprise that it was Christopher.

"What are you doing here?" she asked.

"I might ask you the same." He was suspicious. She had been avoiding him. Why? "You have a bed at the inn. Why are you sleeping on a couch in the tiring-room?"

She averted his stare. "I . . . I had to study some lines . . ."

"Lines." He didn't believe her. Not because that wasn't part of an actor's routine, but because of the manner in which she turned her head so that he couldn't look into her eyes. "There is something else. What?"

She sat up. "I have been thinking about what happened between us the other night and have decided that it just won't work."

He was taken aback. "What!"

She had to protect him at all cost, and lying seemed to be the only way. Otherwise his manly pride would goad him into seeking Jonathan out, an act that would seal his fate. The reward for heroes often was death.

"I find now that I am immersed in my life among the players, 'tis I who need freedom."

"Freedom!" The word so often spoken by him now sounded brash to his ears. "And you think I would not give you that?"

She feigned an anger she did not feel. "I do! Look for example at how you came bursting in here, questioning my whereabouts as if I need to explain my being here to you!"

He looked properly chastised. "Ah, yes. I have to admit that I was wrong." To make amends he said, "But only in my jealousy and anger at thinking I might find you here—"

"With another man?"

"Aye!" He reached for her hand, gently tracing the lines on her palm with his finger. "I am a fool to let passion blind me so, but 'tis because I want our lives to be entwined, Kimberly. I want your face to be the last I see before I sleep and the first I glimpse when I wake."

"Sweet words . . ." And words she had so longed to hear. For just a moment she faltered, that is, until her eyes caught sight of a figure lurking in the shadows. Jonathan! "But words that are too late spoken."

"Too late . . . ?" He was puzzled. Why had she been so warm and loving only to turn cold? What had happened in the interim?

"Aye, 'tis too late to rekindle passions that have long since died." Abruptly she turned her back on him.

" 'Tis over then before it has begun?" He felt betrayed.

She felt her heart break. "Aye," she whispered. "Goodbye, Christopher. I wish you well."

There had been something strange in her expression, something about her words that did not ring true. Although she was a fine actress, she was not so skilled that she could hide the pain that had flickered in her eyes.

"Wish me well?" He took her hand again. "Forsooth you might as well condemn me to Newgate as to wish me gone, for without you my life bodes ill."

She winced, pulling away. "Nevertheless, I do so wish. . . ."

She was acting trapped, cornered, much as she had the night her uncle had been killed. Christopher remembered having caught sight of that infamous gentleman at the theater. Had It been an illusion or reality? Moreover, was it a coincidence that he had sighted the man and now Kimberly was acting like this? That Harold Bowen might somehow be the cause of her strange behavior occurred to him.

"Your uncle!" he blurted out, pulling her to her feet. He started to tell her of his having witnessed the innkeeper at the theater, but his story was interrupted when Jonathan Fairfax came upon the scene. "You!"

"Me!"

There was malice in the way they acted toward each other. Because of her? Kimberly sensed that something else was involved.

"You have no claim to her. 'Tis I who hold her heart."

"Once perhaps." Jonathan looked toward Kimberly, a warning in his expression. "But no more, for I have captured that most worthy prize and will guard it with my life, else my lady Tremaine might end up shattered like another we both know."

Christopher cocked his head. "Another . . . ?"

Jonathan spit the name out. "Angela. Angela Morgan."

"Angela." A name from his sordid past. Christopher winced, remembering the tavern wench he had bedded, then tossed aside. Much to his remorse the pretty, buxom girl had been found floating facedown in the Thames. Suicide? It had been deemed to be so, a supposition that had haunted him for months. "Angela," he said again. "What was she to you?"

Jonathan's eyes flashed. "She was my . . . my cousin."

"Cousin?" Christopher suspected that she had been much, much more. A lover perhaps. "Then I must pay my respects and tell you that her death was through no fault of mine."

"Not yours?" His glare declared otherwise. "She was with child."

"With . . . ?" On his fingers Christopher counted up the time from their last passionate encounter until her death. He shook his head. "I doubt that it was mine . . ."

"You lie! You treated her most brutally, then tossed her aside. A habit that I have heard is just your style. Is it not?"

Christopher's face flushed, a muscle in his jaw ticking dangerously. " 'Tis no business of yours."

"Scoundrel!"

"Churl!"

"Braggart!"

Like two soon-to-be-fighting hounds, they faced each other, hurling insult after insult and epithet after epithet. Teeth bared, fists up, they made preparations to fight.

"No!" Kimberly's command came out as a scream for another such fight had flashed before her eyes. Fearfully she glanced at the wall on which the swords used in the performances were hung. They were dull but might well cause injury.

Christopher saw the direction of her gaze and knew the cause of her fears. "Do not worry. I will not—"

"Slay me as you did that poor unfortunate innkeeper?" Jonathan grinned. "Aye, Christopher, I know your little secret. Indeed, I know all."

Dangerous knowledge for an enemy to have, Christopher thought. Still, he was suddenly relieved for he now realized why Kimberly had shunned him. "So, blackmail it is," he whispered.

"Call it what you will!"

"And just what is the price for your silence?" As if he didn't know.

"You will keep away from Velvet!" Jonathan smiled triumphantly.

"Or . . . ?"

Jonathan shrugged. "I will leave it up to you to provide an answer."

Kimberly's eyes met Christopher's, voicing a silent plea that now was not the time to force the issue.

"I think I can guess," Christopher said dryly. Ordinarily he would have felt bested, might have even had felt a twinge of apprehension. As it were, however, he had to suppress a smile. Harry Bowen wasn't dead. He was certain of it in his heart, his mind, his very bones. It had been no mirage that he had glimpsed from the stage but a man of flesh and blood, a man who was in league with Jonathan Fairfax in some way. Ah, but he would not allow them to win, nor would he cower. He would fight for the woman he loved. First, however, he had to find Harry Bowen somehow, in some way.

Later as he hurried back to his room, Christopher thought about how he could locate Kimberly's uncle in a city as large and heavily populated as London. It would be like looking for a needle in a haystack, especially now that Jonathan had made mention of the incident at Reedham.

"I'll get help from Richard and from the other actors. Somehow we will find the ghoulish bastard." Then and only then would he and Kimberly have any hope for happiness.

Meanwhile he would keep his frustration under control by busying himself with production of his play. At last *The Tragedy of the Highwayman* was going to be staged, with Christopher in the role of Gentleman James. Richard Fletcher had been picked to act the part of the highwayman's stalwart friend Tobias, and John Franklin, a tall hawk-nosed newcomer to the group, had been chosen to play the infamous Scar.

Taking the steps two at a time, Christopher thought of a dozen changes he wanted to make in the final script. Perhaps Richard was right. Perhaps he should have the play end on a positive note. After all, it had been nine years since the highwayman had been hung, and during that time a great many injustices had been righted. Charles was back on the throne, the Royalists had been rewarded for their loyalty to the Stuarts, the theaters had been restored and the style of life was more carefree. Indeed, even Gentleman James's daughter, Devondra, whose husband, Quentin Wakefield, was one of the King's councillors, felt at peace now that the country had returned to normalcy.

He mentally toyed with a way to end the play with Gentleman James still alive as he headed through the door to his room. Perhaps he could have him recite his soliloquy in a cell at Newgate, thus allowing hope for his rescue. Or perhaps he could add a scene wherein the dashing highwayman looked down from heaven, welcoming the return of the King. Perhaps . . .

"What . . . !"

Christopher gasped as he noted the shambles his room was in. Chairs were tipped over, his garments were flung all over the floor. Most worrisome of all, the linen had been stripped from his bed, exposing the mattress wherein he had kept his manuscript safe from the prying eyes of any who might seek to plagiarize his masterpiece.

Hurrying forward, he soon found his worst fears had been realized. "Gone, b'God!"

It was true. He had been robbed of something more precious than money. The manuscript of *The Tragedy of the Highwayman* was missing.

The actors were as colorful a group as could ever be imagined, dressed as they were in multicolored jackets, breeches and feathered hats. Even so, it was a somber group that met with Christopher in the inn's courtyard.

"Stolen, b'God," John Franklin exclaimed, voicing aloud the reason for the meeting. "Need we wonder by whom?"

"Cowards! Thieves," Richard Fletcher scoffed, his eyebrows meeting together in a V. He looked as if he wanted to pick a quarrel, and indeed he did.

"Even If they feared we would steal away their audience, it was no excuse for their thievery," Robert Vickery exclaimed, making no secret of whom he meant by "they," the acting company that made Salisbury their home.

"I would think the theft of my script is personal," Christopher shot back "As to the culprit, I have no doubt but that Jonathan Fairfax is his name."

"Fairfax?" John Franklin was shocked. "Indeed, I am surprised he would be smart enough to look within the mattress for your treasure."

"I'm not surprised," one of the young actors said mockingly. "Forsooth, I would imagine 'tis to a mattress that one's brain would take him."

"Aye, but he will pay!" Christopher exclaimed. "Which is why I called you all together." With an actor's eloquence, he explained to them all that had happened at Reedham, about Jonathan's threat and about his having sighted Harold Bowen from the stage. "I need your help in finding him again, so that this matter of Reedham can be put to rest. Will you aid me?"

There was a mumble of assent.

"One of ours is in trouble. How can we do otherwise?"

"We'll stand behind you, Christopher!"

"If we must look in every corner of London, we'll find him."

# *Seventeen*

Little did Kimberly realize when she first joined the actors just how quickly her reputation would spread. Though there were other actresses in London, it was she who held the hearts of the audience. Even Charles II had taken note of her performance and had expressed interest in meeting her.

Kimberly's appearance in any play sparked such excitement, in fact, that Jonathan insisted on creating a new persona for her. She was to be the daughter of an impoverished Royalist who had escaped from Cromwell by sailing to the new world only to fall victim to an Indian's arrow.

Kimberly thought the story much too fanciful, yet to her surprise the Londoners believed what the handbills said. Now they viewed her as a heroine by manner of her parentage. Little did they know that Jonathan was watching her like a hawk, reminding her over and over again of Christopher's precarious situation. Only by devoting all her energies to acting was Kimberly able to forget her heartache, at least for a while.

She should have been on top of the world, instead she was miserable, haunted by her sense of loss, her yearning for the contentment she had come so close to achieving. Christopher was the only man she wanted, but while he was in London, he might as well have been as far away from her as the stars.

Turning from the window, she looked in the silver mirror, regarding the woman who looked back at her. Sleep had been eluding her all these nights, its lack marking her face with dark circles and frown lines. She had become paler and thinner from worrying about Christopher.

"Miss Tremaine. Velvet." A loud knock on the door accompanied the voice. Answering the summons, Kimberly was surprised to see one of the younger actors in the company.

"Jacob!" By the look on his face she could tell that something had happened. Fearing the worst she grabbed his sleeve. "What is it?"

"The . . . the King! He . . . he's at the theater, and he is demanding to see you."

"To see me?" It wasn't time for the performance. Even so, one did not say no to Charles. Assuring Jacob that she would be at the Salisbury as soon as she could, she closed the door.

But I don't want to go, she thought. She knew just what to expect. The king was a womanizer. He would try to get her alone, and if he succeeded he'd pinch and he'd paw. Men were the same, whether young or old, rich or poor. Except Christopher. When he had touched her it was as if the whole world had dropped from beneath her feet and left her balancing on the edge of a precipice. Sharply she remembered waking up in his arms, feeling his kisses upon her face, her hair.

Closing her eyes, she was troubled by a vision of Jonathan dressed in the robe of a judge, condemning her to a life without the man she loved, a life all alone. There was a cold, sick feeling in the pit of her stomach. She couldn't go on like this! Somehow she had to get free of Jonathan. But how? Enlist the help of the king? It seemed to be the only way.

With renewed vitality, she hurried to the closet and burrowed through her garments, deciding on a velvet gown of emerald green edged in lace. She chose two pieces of jewelry, a rope of pearls and pearl earrings. She would look elegant but not gaudy.

This time when she studied herself in the glass she looked younger, carefree. A mischievous smile lit up her face. Once at her uncle's inn she had planned an escape, but had lost her courage. She wouldn't be a coward this time. Christopher's life might well depend on it.


The presence of Charles II seemed to transform the theater into a royal chamber. Voices buzzed, people scurried to and fro, and heads bobbed up and down as everyone anxiously sought to please the king, a tall bewigged man with an overly long nose who was surrounded by a small knot of men.

"The King!" Even though she had thought herself prepared for this meeting, Kimberly became weak in the knees. She wasn't prepared at all, yet how could she run away?

The answer was that she couldn't. The King's eyes had searched for her and found her. Now, with a grim smile, he beckoned her forward. "Mistress Tremaine," she thought she heard him say.

Hesitantly she stepped forth, her eyes averted from his face. Pausing before him, she curtsied gracefully, much as she did before the audience at the end of a performance. And all the while the only thing she could really see were the square toes of his black leather shoes. "Your Majesty."

"Ah, Mistress Tremaine!"

She raised her head. His face was very near to hers as he bent over her. His small dark eyes were cold, his mouth beneath the small black mustache left little doubt as to what he wanted of her, indeed of all women.

"Your Majesty," she said again.

"Ah no, call me Charles," he implored. He extended his hand, catching hers in a gentle clasp and raising it to his lips. "I've been waiting a long time to meet you."

"Have you, Ch-Charles?" Kimberly studied the man intently, trying to assess his character. He was tall, at least to her, a slender man with shoulder-length dark hair that was tightly curled. From collar to well-polished shoes he was well dressed, in a red velvet jacket, white lace shirt and black knee-length breeches.

"It is an honor to have you with us. I hope you will make yourself at home for our performance."

"Indeed, I will."

The manner in which he was looking at her seemed to strip Kimberly naked. Uncomfortable and nervous, she was also angry because no king—no man—had a right to assume that any woman was his for the taking. Surely *she* was not!

"You're beautiful. Rumor has not done you justice." His eyes were riveted on her face. "I must have a portrait painted of you."

To hang on a wall beside the rest of his conquests, Kimberly thought with an indignant sniff. A chill seeped into her bones as she wondered what would happen if she refused. She stiffened. The last thing she needed was her portrait hanging on a wall for all to view. Certainly she and Christopher were in enough trouble.

"Thank you for the compliment, but there are other actresses in England. . . ."

"None as fair as you. . . ." His gaze caressed her with a familiarity that made her blush. Oh, she knew that look all right, and knew it boded ill. The men at her uncle's inn had stared at her with this same familiarity. Before Kimberly could protest he had taken her by the fingers, placing her hand in the crook of his arm as they made their way toward the stage. Certainly it was proving to be an uncomfortable situation.

"Wait, your Majesty!"

Though usually she had little liking for his presence, Jonathan for once saved the day. Running up beside her, he quickly settled himself at Kimberly's other elbow, yearning to earn the favor of the King.

Charles's eyes sparked with annoyance. "And just who is this—this overeager spaniel?"

"Romeo," Kimberly said sarcastically by way of introduction.

"Jonathan Fairfax!" Jonathan corrected stubbornly.

The King didn't seem to care, saying in Kimberly's ear,

"I've always been a man who enjoys a chase. It makes the prize more worthwhile." His smile was most engaging, giving her a glimpse of the man who had charmed many women.

"Alas, I fear that I am not a prize available for the taking."

The words were spoken before they could be left unsaid and were answered by the loud gasp that shuddered through the huge room. All eyes turned toward Charles as the assemblage awaited his reaction to her rebuff.

Charles didn't even flinch. "And just why is that?" he asked.

Kimberly's eyes were wide with unabashed honesty. "Because I am deeply in love with someone else."

Again there was a gasp, followed by a long seemingly endless silence, but although Kimberly feared a severe reprimand, such punishment was not forthcoming. Instead, Charles seemed more intrigued. "Alas, an honest woman with the courage to speak what is on her mind." He laughed softly. "I envy your lover, madame. If only I had met you first." He whispered in her ear, "Would I have had a chance then?" He answered his own question. "Nay, for I can see in your eyes that despite your profession you are not a woman who tarries lightly, or who gives her heart easily."

"Nay, I am not." Strange how she suddenly felt so at ease with him.

"Nor are you one who would give idle compliments just to earn my favor." He obviously respected that. "Nonetheless you have earned it." Reaching for her hand again, he gave it an affectionate squeeze. "If ever you have the need, I will grant you one favor."

It was a promise Kimberly took to heart.

# *Eighteen*

The actors had staunchly vowed to help him, and Christopher was grateful. He blessed them, each and every one. If he hadn't known it before, he was now assured that Richard Fletcher, Robert Vickery, Jonathan Franklin and the others were more than just stage companions, they were friends.

Fletcher had, in fact, wasted little time in posting four of the younger actors as lookouts—in the hallway, at the front door and the back. "Aye! We must do whatever it takes," he had said.

"Let us, each and every one, keep an eye out for this scoundrel who amuses himself by playing dead. It appears that he is the key to proving Christopher's innocence," Vickery exclaimed.

"Of course!" Richard Fletcher stroked his mustache. "If we could capture the rascal we might be able to force an apology from him."

"Aye. If I know human nature," John Franklin interjected, "and I do, he will haunt our London, perhaps our very audience in the hope of catching sight of Christopher again. And when he does we will seize *him*." The suggestion caused the actors to lapse into a frenzy of plotting and planning.

Still, reality had intruded all too harshly in their make-believe sphere, reminding them of just how fragile a man's destiny could be. Beyond the perimeters of the stage was a real world that far surpassed in harshness, deception and social ambition anything that Shakespeare could create for his tragedies.

That afternoon at the performance the mood was somber as the actors looked out at the crowd that was elbowing each other for space. Over and over again in their minds they recalled the description Christopher had given them. Could they find Bowen? After all, the man was fairly ordinary, with no special scars, marks or freckles to distinguish him.

Christopher felt certain of victory, yet his optimism dwindled as *All's Well That Ends Well* began and he stepped upon the stage to speak his lines. Harry Bowen wasn't in the crowd. He had been foolish to think life could be so simple.

" '. . . I must attend his majesty's command, to whom I am now in ward, evermore in subjection,' " he declared to the actor who played Lafeu, an old lord.

Christopher knew the plot of the play backwards and forwards. After curing the king of a malady, Helena, the daughter of a famous physician, is rewarded by the king's giving her in marriage to Bertram, the character Christopher played. He, however, scorns her and departs for the Florentine war. Only when Helena fulfills his terms will she win his love.

Nonetheless, for the first time in his career Christopher was nervous as the play proceeded. Although it was a comedy he was little inclined to laugh. Doubts haunted him. What if he was wrong about having seen Harold Bowen? What if the man really had been killed that night and it was but his ghost that had come. What if . . . ?

He stiffened as he caught sight of a familiar gray-haired, head. Was he seeing things, or was Harold Bowen among those seated in the gallery? Squinting his eyes, he looked hard and long at the tavern keeper deciding at once that it was he.

" 'It may be you have mistaken him, my lord.' " No, as the tall, skinny figure turned his head, Christopher knew that it was him. Ghoulish to the end, he had come. Like some evil ghost, he was haunting the acting company with his presence. But why?

"Oranges. Ripe and juicy, oranges." An orange girl paused directly in front of Kimberly's mean-spirited uncle.

"B'God, girl, move out of the way. You are blocking my view of the stage!" Bowen's quarrelsome voice carried with all the volume of an actor's.

"Yes, my lord." Bowing her head in a proper show of deference the girl hurried to obey, though she didn't move very far. Christopher's gaze went from the stage to the audience, then to Harold Bowen. For a long time he just stared at him, watching as the man lifted his hand to his nose to stifle a sneeze.

"Ahem . . ."

Christopher tensed, then realizing the other actor had just given him a cue to his line, he called out, " 'Sir, it is a charge too heavy for my strength; but yet we'll strive to bear it, for your worthy sake, to the extreme edge of hazard.' " Beneath his breath he whispered to Richard Fletcher, "He's there! Up in the gallery. Next to the orange seller."

Those words were repeated from Fletcher to Vickery to the young actor whose job it was to go in search of the tavern keeper.

From his position on stage Christopher watched as a rival play unfurled in the gallery. He saw the young actor lunge, saw Harold Bowen duck out of his grasp. Taking a step forward, the innkeeper stumbled, tipping a basket of oranges as he fell against the pretty orange seller. The colorful fruits went everywhere, scattering in a myriad of directions.

"Oh, my oranges!" The girl's wail was unnerving.

Nearly every head in the gallery turned to get a glimpse of what was going on, watching in avid fascination as the young actor struck out with his fists. This time, however, Harold Bowen was in no mood to fight. With a loud shout decrying the young actor's parentage, he took to his heels.

From his place on the stage, Christopher watched with hammering heart, forgetting a line here and there as he silently coached the young pursuer. Then, just as he recited " 'What shall be done to him,' " he saw to his relief that Harold Bowen had been caught. From the audience two other actors came forward to guard him.

" 'Nothing, but let him have thanks. Demand of him my condition, and what credit I have with the duke,' " came the answering line.

It had worked. Thanks be to the actors, the plan had gone much smoother than he had ever dared hope. Now, if only he could contain his impatience until the end of the play.

" 'Nay, by your leave, hold your hands; though I know his brains are forfeit to the next tile that falls . . .' "

Never had a performance passed so slowly. As if in slow motion the actors moved about the stage, reciting their lines. At last, however, they were taking their bows. Then and only then was Christopher free to slip away. Jumping from the stage, he ran to the gallery and climbed up the pole.

"Aha! So, you think to torment me by playing ghost," he scolded.

Leaning forward, he stared Harold Bowen full in the face in a gesture meant to be intimidating. It was Christopher, however, whose mouth dropped open, for it was not Harold Bowen scowling back at him but someone else. Someone he recognized all too well.

"Jonathan Fairfax!" Costumed in a gray wig, false nose and dun-colored coat and pants, the actor looked perilously like Kimberly's uncle. But why was he dressed this way? What strange charade was being played?


Like a snarling wolf, Jonathan struggled against the arms that held him. "So, now you know. Let me go."

Christopher clenched his teeth, shaking his head. No, b'God, he wasn't going to make it that easy. Jonathan Fairfax would pay dearly for this deception.

"You have no right to hold me. I am no criminal."

"Oh?" Christopher's eyes flashed sparks. "Perhaps not, and

yet impersonating a dead man might be deemed by some to be suspect."

"A jest upon you, that is all!" Jonathan Fairfax protested. "Hardly a deed to put me behind Newgate's walls."

What a malicious joke it had been. That it was a joke at all, Christopher doubted.

"Murder, however, is."

"Murder!" Once again the accusation had been leveled against him. "I did not—"

"You're nothing but gibbet bait, Christopher."

"I'm an honorable man. An actor of great reknown."

"You are a man who, by his own words, rode the Heath with a highwayman." Jonathan grinned again.

" 'Twas *you* who stole my play!" And the notes with the script. Notes that revealed intimate details of Christopher's former life. Now he knew it was for a much more sinister reason than plagiarism the play had been taken.

"I needed evidence so that I could prove what kind of man you are."

"Evidence . . . ?"

"The worm has turned, and you are the one who has been cornered. Now it's only a matter of time before you are dangling from a rope."

"Hang? Me?" Though he sounded confident, Christopher paled for just a moment. The hideous death suffered on the scaffold was brutally painful, as well he knew.

"Yes, hang!" Jonathan countered. "I have been in contact with several men from Reedham, witnesses as it were."

"Liars, you mean." Realizing that their conversation was being overheard, Christopher turned to the others. "You must listen to me, kind people. I have done no wrong. 'Twas self-defense and nothing sinister."

There was mumbling as heads were nodded.

"Save *your* lies." Jonathan played the tiny audience with an actor's skill. "This man tried to run off with a tavern keeper's niece. When that man tried to guard his ward's honor, he was cruelly set upon and murdered."

"I didn't—"

"You did! They saw you."

Christopher followed the direction of Jonathan's pointed finger. Standing by the edge of the stage were two portly men he recognized all too well. They were from Reedham, and he could only guess at the reason for their presence.

The moon was full, a large glowing ball in the black sky when Christopher sought out Kimberly at the inn. The inn yard was silvered with the moon's muted radiance as she returned from the theater. Startled by the figure that blocked her way, she was frightened at first, that is, until she recognized him. "Christopher!"

"He's won!"

"Jonathan."

He nodded. "He has made the acquaintance of two men from Reedham who frequented your uncle's tavern and were there that night."

"No!" It was much worse than she ever could have feared. "Our price for relishing fame."

His hand moved to her chin, then trailed softly to her throat. "No, the price we pay for loving each other. 'Tis jealousy that goads Jonathan on and nothing else."

They stared at each other, two dark silhouettes entwined against the curtains of the window. Christopher's face was stony, his expression difficult to read. Was it any wonder then that a knot tightened in the pit of Kimberly's stomach? "What . . . what are we going to do?"

"Not we. Me!" He took a deep breath, knowing full well that she would not like what he was going to say. "I must leave London immediately, otherwise I just might end up in Newgate."

"No!" she gasped. She couldn't bare the thought of his leaving. "We'll go together, just as we did that night when we left Reedham." Reaching out, she touched his dark hair, brushing it back from his face.

He smiled as he remembered the wagon and how steadfastly she had clung to the reins in her effort to save him. Still, he knew he had to leave her behind once again.

"You are an actress of great reknown. I don't want you to become a fugitive on account of my rash actions." It seemed the years had come tumbling down upon him and he was already an old man. He gazed intently at Kimberly, wanting to engrave every detail of her beauty upon his memory. The arching of her brows, the upward tilt of her mouth, the way the moonlight danced upon her pale golden hair.

Kimberly took a deep breath. There was something magical about their surroundings. The grass seemed to sparkle with diamonds, the branches of the trees were entwined as if embracing, the breeze seemed to be humming a love song. It was a night for lovers, not a night for saying goodbye.

"Rash actions?" She remembered how he had stood up to her uncle. He had been a hero, fighting for her honor. How then could she desert him now? "Brave I would say."

"Whatever you want to call them, I don't want to hurt you."

"Then don't go without me. I love you, Chris . . . ."

His mouth came down and smothered the sound of his name. His kiss was fierce, unleashing the torment of his emotions. He took her breath away, held her lips captive to an assault that was unlike anything Kimberly could ever have imagined. The hard, warm length of him was against her, heating her body with a fire that made her burn.

One of his hands slid over the curve of her hip, pressing her firmly against him as his teeth gently nipped at her lips; then he melded his mouth to hers once again, kissing her deeply, as if in this one moment he could rob her of her very soul. And so he did! She found herself entering another realm, a place where only feelings reigned. And her feelings were all too potent.

When at last he pulled away and she could stare back at him, Kimberly looked deeply into his eyes, determined to delve into his soul as he had tried to do with hers. What she read in his gaze warmed her heart.

"You won't leave me. . . ."

He began mumbling, as much to himself as to her. "He was lunging blindly at me, angered to the point of carelessness. You know. You saw. It was an accident."

"It was self-defense. My uncle was coming at you with the intent to kill. Indeed, I think he would have done so without even a second thought. You have no need to defend yourself to me." She paused, then said, "I met the King today. He befriended me." She put his hand to her lips, kissing it gently. "I'll go to him and ask him for clemency. It will work. You will see."

"You believe Charles will listen?"

"I do. He lived in exile while Cromwell reigned and understands much more than other kings might."

"Then at least I have some hope." He blessed her loyalty, her bravery, but most of all her love. "At least I have that!" There was a price upon his head, he might be betrayed and set upon at any moment, yet he knew that Kimberly believed in him.


They held hands as they walked up the stairs. The interior of the inn was dark. Fumbling with the door, Kimberly pushed it open, then reached for Christopher's hand to pull him inside. "I'll pack quickly," she said. "I'll take only what is necessary."

"I'll do the same, then meet you at the stables." He meant to say goodbye, but the nearness of her was too much for him. He reached out, his hands lingering on the soft curves of her body, and pulled her to him.

"Kimberly! Kimberly! I've waited for you all my life." His lips went across her forehead, brushing gently over her heavy dark lashes, then descending to tease the line of her jaw and finally caressing her neck. "I don't want to let you go!" Emotion caused his throat to tighten, making his voice husky. "I can't."

"Christopher . . ." She lifted her arms to encircle his neck, clinging to him, her breasts pressed against his chest, wishing they didn't have to run away. Damn Jonathan!

Christopher buried his face in the pale cloud of her hair, inhaling the spicy scent she always used. "I wish we had time to make love. I wish . . ."

Mutely Kimberly fought against her tears. She leaned against him, outlining the shape of his mouth with her fingertips. "There will be time, once we have left London, once you are safe."

Regretfully they parted, Christopher saying one last time. "The stables. Half an hour."

The moon was beginning its downward descent as Christopher walked along the cobbled stones on his way back to his own lodging. Strange, he thought, how quickly one's future could change. He had taken the routine of his life so for granted, arising in the morning, dressing, going to the theater. Now suddenly he was leaving the stage and London behind. And yet, tonight while holding Kimberly in his arms, his leaving hadn't really mattered. Perhaps because he realized now that she was his future.

Hurrying through the darkness, anxious to put this "escape" behind him so that he and Kimberly could get on with their lives, Christopher headed toward the three-story, half-timbered, whitewashed inn. During Shakespeare's day the inn had been splendid. Now it was run down, its roof and support beams rattling from decay. Still, it had been comfortable. A home of sorts. Opening the creaking door and stepping into the darkness, he shook his head sadly, saying a silent goodbye to the place, to his friends, to the theater.

Suddenly the darkness was replaced by a flood of blinding light. Squinting, Christopher tried to focus on the man of enormous girth who blocked his way. "Who . . . ?"

The man didn't reveal his identity. Nevertheless a chill crept up Christopher's spine. Somehow he knew.

"Is this him?"

"Aye." Just one word was spoken, yet Christopher recognized the speaker. Jonathan.

"Then I will do my duty."

There was a long pause. Christopher looked left and right, planning his escape. Alas, too late. The door was blocked, and all other avenues of escape were covered by armed men. He was trapped. All he could do was listen helplessly as he heard the words.

"Christopher Sheldon, I arrest you in the King's name."

# Nineteen

Never had an evening passed so slowly. As Kimberly paced about in the stables it seemed that everything and everyone was proceeding in slow motion. Her line of vision was directed at the door as she waited for Christopher to come. Where was he? How long could it possibly take to pack? Why hadn't he come back for her?

Listen to me. I sound like a nagging wife, she thought in self-condemnation. She had to be patient. Christopher would have an explanation. Perhaps he had been cornered by one of the actors, she knew how they all loved chitchat. He would have to be careful not to alert anyone that something was wrong. He'd talk awhile, then hurry upstairs. She shouldn't be impatient. And yet . . .

Tonight, just as on many other evenings, she had had the eerie feeling that Jonathan watched over her. She wanted to be away from here, away from London and the dangers it presented. "Oh, Christopher, hurry!"

Was it stuffy in the stables, or were nerves making her so uncomfortable? Pausing beside the door, she lifted her thick hair from her nape to cool her soft skin, taking time to peer out the window. Though men came and went, there was no sign of Christopher.

She paced, she swore, she looked out the stable door a dozen times or more. At last she could stand it no longer. Going out the door, she ran all the way to his inn. Making her way to

Christopher's room, she knocked. There was no answer. She knocked again. It was silent inside. Anxiously she peeked within, hoping against hope that somehow she would find him there. The room was empty.

"What if I missed him. What if we took different paths and he is now waiting for me at the stables?" It was such a disastrous thought that she gasped. So much for impatience. "But what if . . . ?"

She refused to listen to the voice within that whispered he wasn't coming back, that he had deserted her once again. He wouldn't do that, not this time, she told herself. Not after what they had shared. He loved her. He'd proven it with his gentle hands and soft words. No, she had missed him, that was all. It was dark. He had taken another path . . .

"He's gone!"

Jonathan's voice startled her.

"He left in quite a hurry. So much of a hurry that I doubt he'll ever be back." He laughed. "Now why is that? Some dark secret, do you suppose?"

"He hasn't left!"

Taking a deep breath she reached for the doorknob and pushed, opening the door wide. It was dark inside the room, but the opening in the curtains let in just enough moonlight to reveal that the room was quite empty. His boots, hats, shirts, breeches and satchels were missing. The room was, in fact, picked clean of his belongings.

"How could he?" Tears stung her eyes. Disappointment and heartache threatened to choke her. The thought that she had been left behind nearly destroyed her. He had gone, and she didn't even know where he was going. How would she find him?

"He left you behind with only this to console you." Jonathan dangled a piece of paper in front of her eyes.

Christopher had left a note. She reached out, but Jonathan snatched it away.

"Oh, no! Not so easily." His eyes hardened as he grabbed her arm. "There's a price to be paid for this."

"A price?" Kimberly's blood ran cold. Just what did he mean?

"A kiss." His thin lips curved upward to reveal his flawless smile.

"No!"

"Yes." His eyes narrowed in the manner she knew meant he was angered.

"No! Don't touch me!" Kimberly put up a hand to fend him off, but he was much stronger than he looked. With an oath he pulled her to him. "Please!"

"Please," he mocked.

Struggling against him, Kimberly tried to break his grip, but he held her securely. "Christopher will have your head for this. When he comes back he'll—"

"Back? He's not coming back? Not according to his little note."

Jonathan took great satisfaction in reading it to her. Christopher said that although he'd enjoyed their moments together, and he'd found her most desirable, he must leave her behind. He wished her happiness in the future with a suitable husband, which he most certainly would never be.

"He's gone," Jonathan said again.

A frightening premonition edged its way up Kimberly's spine. She found it difficult to think, difficult to speak. "Jonathan. What have you done?" She cast a bone-chilling stare on the man she had once considered a friend.

"I . . . ?" He feigned innocence.

"Where is Christopher?" A sick feeling was burgeoning inside her stomach. "What have you done, Jonathan?"

He didn't answer, but his self-righteous expression told the story for him. Stubbornly he pursed his lips.

Kimberly couldn't stem the murderous rage that consumed her. There was a roaring in her ears. Blindly she hurled herself at him, forgetting for the moment that she was a lady. They rolled down the stairs to the bottom of the carpeted landing.

"You selfish oaf! You'll be sorry if you have harmed Christopher in any way." A part of her was screaming in silent anguish. A part of her already knew. "Where is he?"

Jonathan made a brutal confession. "I turned him in. He's at Newgate where he belongs."

"Newgate!" She felt hot, she felt cold. She fought to get to her feet, but suddenly she couldn't move. "No!"

Jonathan laughed. "A clever way to get rid of the competition. No?"

"No . . . !"

Kimberly raced to the door, calling Christopher's name, at the top of her lungs, as if he could hear her. But she told herself that wouldn't do any good. She must not lose her wits. She had to keep calm. She had to do everything in her power to free Christopher. But how? What power had she?

The King! Charles's face flashed before her eyes.


It was hot in the windowless cell. So hot that Christopher Sheldon had stripped down to his underwear in an attempt to make himself comfortable. Worse yet, the stale odor of rotting straw assailed his nostrils as he looked about him at the cold stone walls of his prison cell. Newgate. The most frightening nightmare of all.

He remembered all too vividly his humiliating ride in the prison cart. He had been shackled, treated most wretchedly. And Jonathan Fairfax's laughter had rung in his ears on the long, bumpy ride to the prison.

They had had to drag him from the cart and had thrust him up the stairs. Oh, he had been stubborn, a snarling, swearing, fighting bear as they'd half carried, half pushed him toward the scarred doors. Somberly he had watched as the guard had recorded his name in the large leatherbound prison book. Christopher Sheldon he had written. A name once reknowned and now defiled. And all because of Jonathan Fairfax. Oh, how he detested him!

"So, you are Christopher Sheldon, are ye?" The guard seemed to recognize the name.

"I am. The actor."

"Actor." The guard hesitated. "Why, I saw you in *The Merchant of Venice*."

"You might have, had I been in it," Christopher had mumbled. It was perhaps the only play he had never been in.

"Aye, I remember now." The stocky guard had guffawed. "You played Jessica."

"Very funny!" Christopher wondered if this simpleton had ever seen the inside of a theater. If he had, he would know that men rarely played women's roles anymore. "In reality I played Lady MacBeth!"

"Aye, I know." The guard grinned. "But you won't be thinking you are royalty now. There isn't any aristocracy here." His voice had lowered conspiratorially. "Unless you have some money stashed away that you could give to old Charlie. I can prove to be a good friend or a powerful enemy. I'll let you choose which it's to be."

Christopher had heard Gentleman James talk about bribery. He knew just what the guard meant. Without paying bribes his life would be hell. " 'Tis a simple decision. I would prefer that you would be my friend."

"Ah now, there is a very smart man." Holding out his hand, the man seemed easy to satisfy, for it took only a few coins.

Christopher had then been led along the dank dimly lit stone passages. A thick iron-hinged door had swung open, and he had been pushed into a stinking cell with a small barred window.

"Caged, b'God." And he knew just where to place the blame. Jonathan Fairfax. Oh, how he would love to get his hands on that bastard! Turned in! Well, Fairfax would pay.

His eyes bright as coals, he was beyond feeling anything but anger. He would be given a trial no doubt. A mockery of justice if ever there was one. And then what? What kind of punishment would there be?

Christopher lay down on a thick pile of moldy straw, stretching out his arms and legs as he contemplated the matter. They wouldn't hang him. Or would they?

"Oh, Kimberly, I had hoped to save you. Now all I can hope for is that you will save me." But how?

London was a seething mass of noise and motion. A commercial center, it was swarming with people. Open carts, coaches, drays, horses and wagons clogged the streets. The waterways, too, were crowded with various types of boats and barges. Even so, it was a lonely world for Kimberly without Christopher, just as she'd known it would be.

There was an ache inside her, a void that nothing and no one could fill. She knew that the players in her company were right when they'd said life must go on. It did. Tediously. Still, the only thing that kept her going was the hope that the King would show clemency.

"Surely there must be some honest man in Reedham, someone who will step forward and tell the truth about what occurred on that fatal day." If not, then she was the only witness in Christopher's defense. Pray God that Charles would believe her.

The voices of the vendors hawking their wares, the church bells, the grumbling of shoppers haggling over the prices of purchases were familiar to Kimberly's ears. Today as she walked along, however, they were unnerving. She wanted to run over so many things in her mind, she needed to remember so many things.

Elbowing her way through a crowd she added her presence to the confusion, crossing the street carefully so as not to be run over by the carts and wagons. Church spires; steeply pitched roofs of three-storied, gabled houses; turreted towers; and trees all formed a jagged landscape against the sky. From chimneys and smokestacks billowed the dark gray smoke originating in the forges and furnaces in the workshops below them. At last, Kimberly could see the square tower of St. Paul's Church reaching toward the heavens, and she imagined that it was saying a prayer that she would be successful in getting Christopher freed.

"Think of this as the most important performance of your life," she told herself. And she knew she was up to it. "You can convince the King. You can!"

Only when she saw the walls of Whitehall did she begin to lose her newfound confidence. Putting her hand up to her hair, she brushed back the stray curl that had fallen loose. She wanted to look attractive. Knowing full well that Charles had an eye for a pretty face, she had taken a great deal of time with her toilette, attiring herself in one of her better gowns for the audience, a white dress decorated with pearls. White, the color of purity and innocence.

She announced herself to the guard at the front gate and was admitted. Hearing the gate click shut she swallowed hard, but now was not the time to become queasy. She was Christopher's only hope.

Stepping inside the crowded anteroom, she looked about her. It was a bright world she entered, as she had heard it would be. More colorful even than the theater. She was aware of the ladies in their silk, brocade and velvet gowns, jewelry sparkling like stars as they moved about. Their stares were hostile, amused, mocking and curious, but each and every look they gave her emphasized that she was an outsider, an interloper, a rival in their world of pomp and glitter.

Kimberly walked slowly through the rooms hardly even noticing the splendor of the furnishings. Her attention was fixed on the man in the ornate chair at the end of the chamber. Charles II. King. Around him, like planets revolving around the sun, stood a circle of men, their faces marked by expressions of mock adoration. Their flatteries were marked by insincerity.

As Kimberly had entered, these men had shown a faint flicker of interest, furtive glances darting to her on the sly. Merry-go-up. How was she going to get rid of them? She needed to see the King alone. Privacy was important to her plan, for she could not tell all that was needed before other listening ears.

"Aha, a fair butterfly. Have you seen, your Majesty?" One man was not so secretive in his ogling.

"A butterfly?" Charles questioned. At last he looked her way.

Suddenly two of the King's Guards crossed their pikes in front of her. "What is your business?" one of them snarled. Kimberly stated her purpose in coming, then watched as the reason for her visit was announced to the King.

"He says he will see you," came the reply.

Hesitantly at first, then more boldly, she walked forward. Outwardly she was calm, but inside she was trembling as she somehow forced her feet to carry her to where Charles sat. Attired in red velvet and silver cloth, he looked elegant and powerful; still, as she walked forward his smile reminded her of his promise of friendship.

"Ah, so indeed it is a butterfly that makes an appearance here." Seeming to tire of the fawning attention of his male courtiers, he motioned them away.

Kimberly halted. Her heart hammered so in her chest she was certain it would burst. Calling upon all her poise as an actress, however, she dipped into a curtsy, spreading her white skirts like a fan.

The King smiled. "And just what is your reason for requesting an audience?"

Kimberly moved closer. "I come in the name of Christopher Sheldon, your Majesty. He has been dealt a great wrong. I am here to ask for your help."

"What kind of wrong?"

"He has been condemned to Newgate. But he is innocent. I know. I saw." The story tumbled from Kimberly's lips. Providing as many details as she could, she told of her uncle's anger, his insistence that there be a fight. She told of how he had lunged at Christopher.

"And were there other witnesses?"

She nodded. "But that is my fear. They were all friends of my uncle. I do not believe Christopher can possibly have a fair trial.

"Can you . . . can you free him?"

"No. I can not—will not—interfere in the justice system." Charles paused. "However, perhaps if my presence is known, I can make certain that it is a fair trial."

"I see." No acting talent on earth could hide her disappointment.

"Oh, come. Do not look so down in the mouth. It will all work out in the end."

Maybe it would, and maybe it would not. Kimberly's hopes were dashed. She felt deserted and confused as she walked back toward the entranceway. Even so, she knew this was a start. Somehow she would give convincing enough testimony for Christopher to be freed. She must!

# Twenty

Dark walls loomed all around Christopher. Except for the thick wooden door with its tiny grille there was no way to look out. And the prison cell was so small he was beginning to feel boxed in.

Moreover he was being forced to eat disgusting food if he wanted to eat at all, and was made to suffer the utter boredom of this brick-and-stone, stinking prison. He was locked up like a common criminal. Was it any wonder then that his world was slowly crumbling? The only thing that had lifted his spirits was believing he was going to get out, that Kimberly would find a way to save him. Now he was not so certain of that.

"Murder." It was something they stretched a man's neck for while the onlookers chortled and babbled. He would be on stage for one last time, albeit for an ugly, gruesome ending to his life.

The very thought was frightening. Horrifying. Over and over again he remembered how terrible it had been to witness the hangings on Tyburn Hill. He felt helpless. Frustrated. Just when he had found everything he had ever wanted, when life looked as though it was going to end like a well-scripted play, he had been cornered.

Putting his feet on a small, round stool he ran his hands through his stubbled beard. Vanity now was a thing of the past, for who cared a wit about it here? Christopher was consumed by frustration. He had promised Kimberly that he would come back for her, but this unfortunate and dangerous turn had caused him to break his word. All he could hope was that she would somehow learn what had happened to him. He wouldn't want her to think he had deserted her again. Not with Jonathan Fairfax waiting in the wings.

"Psst. Christopher. . . .!" It was Kimberly's voice, coming from outside.

He bolted to his feet and ran to the small barred grille. Clinging to the bars, he looked out at her, laughing softly when he saw that she was standing on a box in order to reach the window.

" 'Romeo, Romeo, wherefore art thou, Romeo,' " he declaimed, mockingly. "Alas, thou art in Newgate. Ah, but a prison by any other name would smell."

" 'As sweet?' " Kimberly finished for him.

He laughed. "Hardly." He let his breath out in a long drawn-out sigh. "What a terrible place."

"I know."

"You haven't perchance brought a saw from the stage master's cupboard have you?"

"A saw?" She gripped the bars, then, reaching out, touched his hand, holding it for a long poignant moment. "No, but I wish I had if it could get you out of here."

He looked terrible. He was pale, and there were dark circles under his eyes.

"With all the guards posted, alas, a saw would not be enough."

"I'm going to get you out of here, Christopher."

"Out?" Christopher was afraid to hope still he asked, "How?"

"I went to see the King."

"And he's given me a pardon!" He gave a shout of joy.

"No!" She condemned herself for having falsely raised his hopes. "But he did say he would make his presence known at the trial."

"At the price of what reward?" he asked jealously. He had

heard about her visit from the King and knew Charles's reputation all too well.

She stiffened. "Not what you think? He was, in fact, most kind to me."

"Kimberly . . ." His whisper asked her forgiveness. "Of course, I meant no insult to you. It is just that the King is known for his obsession with beautiful women."

"Perhaps, but he is also touched by the heart of a woman in love. He told me so."

"Then I thank him." He sighed again. "But I will thank him far more when I am far from here!" For just a moment he walked away from the door. Pacing, he wondered if there was sufficient evidence to convict him. How many witnesses would come forth? And what about the jurors? Perjury and bribery were all too common. Would Jonathan dirty his hands in such a way? Or was there a chance for justice to be done?

"Kimberly . . ." He walked toward the grille again. "If—if the worst happens, if I am condemned, I want you to go to my friend, Richard Fletcher. He will see that you are safe and will be most fair in displaying your talents." He clenched his jaw. "Forsooth, what I am really saying is that I could not bear the thought of you with Jonathan Fairfax. Not after what he has done."

"Never! I would never stay with him." Her voice was choked with misery. "Neither could I live without you, my love."

"You would have to." His voice was husky. "You are a lovely woman. I would want you to marry and have children."

"The theater would be my husband."

"No. 'Tis no kind of life. One day you would grow old. The audience is fickle."

"I can take care of myself."

"You need a man to care for you."

She swallowed her tears. "I want no man but you."

The footsteps of the guard sounded like thunder. "You will have to leave now, miss. You can stay no longer."

Kimberly put her face up to the bars, brushing Christopher's lips with her own. "I will go for now, but my heart will be here with you."

The words echoed in Christopher's mind and brought him a sense of calm as she walked away.

Night was the worst time of the day's cycle for Christopher. It emphasized his loneliness. Aside from the snores coming from the other cells, it was much too quiet. Ominously so. And it was dark in the prison. Only a cracked lamp with a very short wick gave off any light. It was a time of contemplation and a time of agitation.

"If I have to stay here much longer, I swear I will go mad!" He would, he knew it. To guard against lunacy, he marked off the time by reciting all the soliloquys that he could remember. For just a moment he was Hamlet again, then Mark Anthony, then MacBeth.

Another five minutes went by, then another ten. Just when Christopher's spirits were at an all time low and he was preparing to settle himself down in his straw pallet for the night, the guard ushered in a man whose face was as welcome as the sun.

"Richard!"

"Methinks you have taken some lines much too seriously," he grumbled. "Or are you perchance doing research for a play?"

Christopher was not in a mood for humor. "B'God, you know it damned well! That toady, Jonathan Fairfax, has taken it upon himself to get me hung."

Richard sighed wearily. "Indeed, it is beginning to appear that way. Even so, I want you to know that we have not given up looking."

"For Harold Bowen?" His tone was scolding. "That one is dead. I shouldn't have held onto any hope that it would be otherwise."

"Ah, I suppose he is, still it isn't hopeless, Christopher. The other actors and I are checking every nook and cranny for sign of a friendly witness. Vickery even went to Reedham." He stood up on tiptoe. "You look exhausted. Perhaps we should talk about this some other time?"

"No, I want to assess my chances, for if I am not to get out of here, I want to secure Kimberly's future."

"You want me to marry her, is that what you mean?"

It hadn't been, but the idea had some merit. "If I am hung, if there is no future for Kimberly and myself, then I want you to protect her. Indeed, I want you to do anything in your power to see that she is happy."

Richard Fletcher spoke with the passion of one used to being heard and believed. "You won't be hung!" In all the days he'd known Christopher Sheldon, nothing had ever defeated the man. Somehow he couldn't believe that anything ever would now.


Clouds hovered low over the city as Kimberly made her way back to the inn. In order to save time and have hope for a little shelter were it to rain, she hailed a boatman and traveled part of the way by barge. All the while remembering Christopher's words to her that he wanted her to be happy.

"I will only be content once I have gotten him out of Newgate, by force if necessary," she whispered to herself, in her daydreams conjuring up visions of a daring rescue. In the end she gave such fantasies up. Christopher was right. Newgate was too heavily guarded for any foolish attempt. Besides, such an act would only make him look more guilty. It seemed, therefore, that the only answer lay in a fair trial, if such a possibility existed.

Perhaps the people of London, the ones he has entertained, will be on his side? Perhaps people would not be as heartless this time as they had been in the past. Perhaps they would be for Christopher and not against him.

As cold drops stung the back of Kimberly's neck, she

glanced up at the clouds. It looked threatening. Turning up the collar of her cloak, she paid the boatman, then ran down the cobbled streets, ducking in and out of shelter as she made her way back to the inn. She was greeted at the front door by an inquisitive group of actors who were nearly as concerned about Christopher as she was.

"How is he? Does he have gaol fever yet?"

Kimberly's dejected look answered for her. "He will soon if not freed."

Edward Mattingly, one of the young actors shook his head. " 'Tis a pity."

A mist left by the rain caressed Kimberly's face, making it sparkle. "He looks thinner and so tired," she answered. Rain dripped from her sodden cloak and she hurried to hang it on one of the pegs by the door.

Two of the actors spoke at the same time. "Newgate is a wicked place."

"The food alone is enough to make one shudder."

Edward had an idea. "Let's get together some food, the inn's best, and take it to him. That should cheer him up."

Kimberly smiled through her tears. "It would."

"Then let's get started . . ."

"Hold!" Sweeping through the doorway, Jonathan held up his hand. "Why trouble yourselves so. Christopher is a doomed man."

"Thanks to you!" Looking into his face, Kimberly wondered how she could ever have thought him to be kind. Obviously he had not a shred of compassion.

"Aye," Edward agreed, "and there is little we can do to help him. Sorry, Velvet."

"Ah, but there is. We can rally the city of London to Christopher's side, we can—"

"Make yourselves the target of scorn when he is found guilty." Jonathan looked so self-righteous it was all Kimberly could do to hold her temper.

Following the others into the main room, she ignored

Jonathan and asked her friends in the company to move among
the citizens and let the injustice of Christopher's story be told.

"He is innocent! I saw. I know!"

"Innocent!" Jonathan glowered at her. "A man who by his
own words was once a highwayman has many sins to answer
for. That murder was one of them seems obvious to all but
you. Could it be that love has made you blind, Velvet?"

Jonathan went on to say that if they sided with a murderer,
they would turn all of London against them. He warned that
a once-plentiful crowd would soon dwindle and be gone.

"Our theater will be empty. Ah, but we can entertain the
rats," he chortled, mocking the rodents' squeaks.

Nevertheless, when all was said and done, the actors decided
in Christopher's favor. In spite of the fact that he was from a
rival company, he was one of them by virtue of his profession.

"We're off!" Edward said, showing Jonathan the back of his
hand in a disparaging gesture. "To let the citizens know that
a brilliant talent is in danger of being silenced."

# Twenty-one

The courtroom at Old Bailey was a veritable sea of faces. Jostling each other, people fought for seats that would give them a good view of the proceedings. Christopher stood wearily with three other unfortunates, wondering what the tone of the crowd would be on this day. Would they jeer him or applaud him? Only time would tell. And the judge? That honorable man and the counsel looked grim. Despite their intricately curled white wigs and dark garments, they did, in fact, almost blend in to the crowd.

As Kimberly entered by a side door, she smiled at him, giving him heart for the tedious trial that was about to begin.

God's blood, but she made a pretty sight, and how he wanted to go to her. Instead he must sit and be a part of this mummery, praying that God in his wisdom and mercy would reach out and touch the hearts of those who sat in judgment.

Christopher could only hope the day's beginning wasn't a premonition of things to come. He had been escorted with his two companions past the cells of Newgate, through the yards and out through the heavy iron-studded door into the waiting prison wagons. Then, with several other frightened, dirty and disheveled men and women, he had been brought to Old Bailey for trial.

"Trial, they call it. Ha, says I!" A ragged, gray-haired man standing next to him snorted his disdain. "Don't know why they bother, I don't.'

"Because they want it to look as if there is justice in this world," said another, looking beseechingly in the judge's direction. "I swear, I didn't do it."

"Didn't do it. Ha! Think they will believe you when I do not."

"Hush!" A stern reprimand from the judge silenced the men.

Looking up, Christopher saw the King enter through the large double doors at the far end of the room, making a grand display. All heads turned to look at him. Dressed in black and gold, Charles looked awesome and unfriendly. Christopher wondered if it would matter to the King that he had been a staunch Royalist at a time when the exiled Charles had had need of friends. He doubted it.

In fact a chilling thought ran through his mind. What if the King, given his vanity, assumed that Kimberly would soon be his were Christopher to suddenly disappear from the world? He shuddered, feeling at that moment as if the rope were already around his neck.

"You may begin . . ." The King nodded toward the judge.

The proceedings were conducted with calm indifference, as if merely a matter of business. There was a great deal of form but no compassion, considerable interest but no sympathy. Kimberly watched warily, assessing the judge who sat pompously straight, the Lord Mayor who was presenting an equal measure of dignity, the barrister who seemed anxious for the morning to be over.

The other prisoners were dealt with quickly and efficiently. One unfortunate man causing laughter when he claimed that he was innocent and 'twas a dog had done the deed.

"Dog, indeed."

"Aye, it was. He stole the wallet and not I."

"Because you trained him, is that not so?"

The man shook his head, denying it, but in the end he was sentenced to a term in Newgate, albeit a short one. The other prisoner was condemned to the gallows for his days upon the Heath, an ominous reminder.

"Now, what is your name?" The judge eyed Christopher so sternly he wished suddenly that he had a mirror and a comb. He hoped he did not look as unkempt as the two men standing beside him.

"Christopher Sheldon!"

The judge studied him critically. "Have you any witnesses to speak to your character, sir?"

"I do!" Christopher motioned to Kimberly.

Rising to her feet, she spoke eloquently in defense of Christopher's good name and breeding. She declared him to be a most loyal subject of the King, a Royalist and a staunch defender of England. She started to tell the story of what had happened at Reedham, but the judge silenced her.

"In good time," he said.

Richard Fletcher also spoke in glowing terms about his friend's character, praising him for his valor in fighting for Charles II's return to the throne. And he spoke highly of Christopher Sheldon's talents as an actor, of his honor as a man.

"In all the time I have known him, he has not done a dishonorable thing to any man," he said earnestly.

"Or woman?" Jonathan, who sat smugly behind Kimberly, said.

Several of the actors from Christopher's company then testified to having strong convictions that he was an honorable man. A murderer, most assuredly not, they all said.

Nodding to a clerk who scratched the information down on a long roll of paper, the judge exclaimed, "Now for the witnesses."

What followed was a living nightmare, a mockery of all things decent. Four patrons of Harold Bowen's inn came forward to testify, and all presented the same distorted version of an "innocent and peaceful man's" death.

"Old Harry was but closing down the inn when he was struck down for no reason," one of the men said. "Aye, I remember him wiping his hands on his apron and telling us all that he was glad he could call it a night."

As if they had been carefully coached, the men related how Christopher, who was obviously drunk, had come upon Harold Bowen, handed him a sword and forced him to fight, laughing all the while.

"I will soon bed your pretty whore of a niece, he said."

The judge whispered in the ear of the clerk, telling him to write it all down. "And then . . . ?"

"In order to defend his niece's honor, old Harry lashed out with his sword, poor fool. The next thing I knew he was tumbling to the ground, from his stomach was coming a never-ending stream of crimson."

"Liar!" Bolting to her feet, Kimberly wanted to pounce upon the viper-tongued man. She was silenced, however, and gritted her teeth as the travesty continued.

Christopher's honor was again besmirched as rumors of his having once been a highwayman were revealed. Placed into evidence were his own notes, regretfully in his handwriting. From the back of the room came an old man, insisting he could identify Christopher as having once held up his carriage with the command, "Stand and deliver!"

There was a twitter in the crowd.

"Put that down," said the judge, frowning all the while.

At last Kimberly had her turn to tell of the events that had taken place. "Christopher Sheldon was my rescuer that night and not my tormentor," she began. "My uncle was miserly, sometimes violent and mean. That night he was twisting my arm so hard that I gasped. Christopher merely came up behind my uncle and told him to let me go."

"He interfered?" The judge's very words told her that he was biased.

"He saved me from grievous injury." Taking a deep breath, she continued. "My uncle was infuriated. Stooping to pick up a sword—it belonged to one of the patrons—he goaded Christopher into a fight."

"And Sheldon proceeded, despite the fact that he was an

experienced soldier and more than a match for someone of your uncle's age."

"No!" Kimberly looked at Christopher. "That is to say, he had no choice. My uncle kept lunging at him. Over and over! Then suddenly my uncle was falling." She hurried to say, "Through no fault of Christopher's."

"No fault?" The judge raised his brows.

"You know what I mean." Oh, dear God, she was flustered, so much so that she was ruining everything. Calming herself, she pretended that she was merely reciting the lines of a play.

"My lord, Mister Sheldon is left-handed!" She gestured toward the defendant, thankful that she had suddenly remembered something important.

"And . . ."

"By their own account the witnesses have stated that Christopher picked up his own sword and fought with it by using his right hand!"

"A pertinent point!" The judge nodded. "Write that down!"

"Obviously he did so in an attempt to give my uncle a more than sporting chance."

Kimberly's words were met with applause from the audience, and its members now took turns at making their thoughts on the matter known. One by one they rose to their feet chanting the words, "Not guilty!"

Angrily the judge insisted on silence; still, it had not gone unnoticed that the majority of people in attendance were on Sheldon's side. He turned toward the accused.

"The charge is murder. A most serious charge. How do you plead?"

"Not guilty." A flash of anger made him defiant. "I did not murder Harold Bowen. It was self-defense. I know, I was there. I am innocent, my lord."

The judge raised his brows, obviously anxious to get the matter over and done with and be on with his day. He conferred with the others who sat in judgment, then started to speak. Before he could begin, however, Charles II rose to his feet.

"Might I, too, be a witness?" he said, and without waiting for approval, swept forward.

A witness? The King? For the first time in his life Christopher was rendered speechless.

"As to this young man being a highwayman, I am sure you are of the definite opinion that it has no bearing on this case." He looked straight at the judge. "Many things were said and done while I was in exile, for Cromwell truly put my country into a state of turmoil. Things done before my return to the throne are therefore seen to be irrelevant."

Kimberly's eyes met those of the King, and she smiled.

"As for Harold Bowen being as helpless as has been pretended, I can give proof that indeed he was not!" Snapping his fingers, Charles procured a document from the hands of one of his attendants. "This should be sufficient to put that lie to rest! An oath of allegiance to Oliver Cromwell, signed by Harold Bowen himself."

The people in the courtroom gasped.

"He was no meek innkeeper, you see. Harold Bowen was a captain in Oliver Cromwell's army, an army that fought against *me!*"

In the courtroom was a cacophony of voices as Charles II took his seat.

"Bravo!" Christopher said beneath his breath. In one fell swoop, the King had rendered Harold Bowen the guilty party because of his allegiance to a would-be king and his standing as a traitor. This time, when he looked at Kimberly it was as if the weight of the world had been swept away. He was as good as free. No one, certainly not the judge, would see him hang now.

"Not guilty!"

Kimberly barely heard the judge's decision. She was much too busy seeking her lover's arms. "Oh, Christopher . . ."

"I'm free. Really free. Thanks to you. . . ." Cupping her chin with a hand he bent down and kissed her.

# Twenty-two

It seemed that all of London turned out for the wedding of Christopher Sheldon and Velvet "Kimberly" Bowen, now Tremaine. A shower of flower blossoms fell to the ground like snow. Trumpets blared and voices rose up in shouts, laughter and rejoicing as merrymakers followed the wedding procession down the neatly cobbled streets.

Tremaine and Sheldon, the theater's "royal couple," they were being called. Indeed it had been whispered that Charles II had taken them both under his wing, merging their theatrical companies into one to which he had given a royal license.

The courtyard was so crowded the entire populace of London might well have come to witness the performance of a real-life love story. It was the wedding of the year. Already the audience twittered expectantly.

"Isn't she lovely!"

"Isn't he handsome!"

"Isn't this the perfect ending for a play."

For her wedding dress Kimberly had chosen a square-necked, white brocade gown with puffed sleeves and a long flowing train. A bridal garland of late-blooming flowers adorned her head. Christopher was dressed in blue velvet coat and breeches, along with black leather boots, the tops of which were pulled down to form very deep cuffs about the lower parts of his knees. It was the latest style.

As they rode in Christopher's playwagon to the church, a

small troupe of minstrels preceded them, playing flute, viol, harp and drums. This gave the ceremony a medieval flair.

"I think even Shakespeare in all his glory would have been impressed," Christopher whispered.

When they arrived at the square in front of the church he gathered her up in his arms and carried her up the stone steps of the chapel to the cheers of the crowd.

"Kiss her!" they called out, a request to which Christopher happily complied.

Inside the church, standing side by side, they listened as the minister began the ceremony, joining them, binding them with love. The gold ring touched first one finger and then another, resting at last on the third finger of Kimberly's left hand in an unending symbol of eternity. Then, before all assembled, Christopher kissed her again. Kimberly slid her arms around her husband's neck, relishing the ritual kiss.

"I wish we could slip away," he whispered in her ear when he pulled away. "I have no liking to share you with the crowd. I want you all to myself."

"Why, we have already had our wedding night," she teased. "No doubt you are already tired of me."

"Tired of you?" He nibbled her ear. "That will never happen, my lady. Even when we are old and gray, I will still lust after you."

She laughed, "And I after you. . . ."

Ignoring the ogling of the crowd, he bent his head and kissed the cleft between her breasts. "You taste good, much better than anything the inn's chef may have prepared for the wedding feast."

"Do I?" She tasted the flesh of his neck. "Mmmm, so do you. . . ."

Passion flared between them. Nevertheless they had to suffer the wanting and the longing as the wedding feast proceeded, an assortment of dishes Charles had had his own cook prepare being offered.

Kimberly gestured with a wide sweep of her hand toward

the assorted delicacies spread out upon the tables; roast swan in orange sauce stuffed with almond dressing, venison, plates of steaming vegetables seasoned with herbs, small loaves of various breads and platters of fruit—grapes, apples, plums and pears. For dessert there were pies, cakes and tarts.

Afterward there was dancing, accompanied by drinking and shouted congratulations. Then the newly wedded couple were escorted up the stairs to their nuptial bed as had been the custom since medieval times. Several pairs of eyes expectantly watched as the bride and groom slipped between the covers, but Christopher blocked the door.

"Thank you, my fine friends," he said. When it looked as if they fully intended to escort the married pair all the way to the bed he merely declared, "Custom be damned, we want to be alone." And they soon were.

Christopher's intense gaze clung to her as he beheld her naked beauty. He ran a hand lovingly over the softness of her shoulder, down to the peaks of her full breasts. This was his bride, his mate for ever and ever.

With a quick, indrawn breath, he drew her to his chest, molding his mouth to hers in a sweetly scorching kiss, and his hands stroked her body, gently igniting a searing flame in her. A blazing fire consumed them as their bodies met. With hands and lips and words, they made love.

"I love you, Kimberly, with all my heart."

"Love?" she asked snuggling up against him. "Are you certain it isn't just gratitude? After all, it was my friendship with Charles that saved the day."

He gently tugged at her hair, smiling. "It was, and I must admit to having been jealous for a while."

"Jealous?" She laughed softly, pleased by his confession.

"Ah, but now you are mine and I love you, I desire you, I worship you. I know this." He knew much more as well. Love was something that must be shared. " 'All's well that ends well.' " Touching her lips, he merged her smile with his as he whispered again, "I love you."

# Epilogue—1669

It was a beautiful spring day. The garden in the inn's courtyard was in full bloom, filling the air with a marvelous perfume. "Oh, what lovely flowers!" Kimberly said softly.

"Flowers," repeated the dark, curly-haired boy who stood beside her. "Pretty," he added. Looking up at her, he winked. "Like you, Mama."

"Ah, so already you show promise of being a lady's man." And why not. He was so much like Christopher in every other way, right down to his temper and fierce independence, that she shouldn't have been surprised.

Seeing her smile, the boy smiled too. "You are happy. Me too!"

"I am very, very happy now," she answered. Content. She had everything she had ever wanted, a loving husband, young Chris, and the wonderful, exciting world of the theater.

That was not to say there had not been dangers and hardships along the way. Two tragedies had struck London without warning. One year after she and Christopher had gotten married the Great Plague had broken out in the city. Only by taking Kimberly with him to the country was Christopher able to save her life, their unborn child's and his own.

One year later London was in flames. The dry season's parched shrubbery and the wooden buildings had fed the ravaging fire. Rumor had hinted that the Great Fire was started by a carelessly handled lantern in one of the theaters but it was never proven. Whoever had been responsible, London had burned to the ground, as had its theaters. Now everything was being rebuilt. This time the buildings would be of stone, including the new theater.

"Look, Mama, a rose," Chris declared merrily.

"Which by any other name would smell as sweet." Coming up behind them, Christopher was the very picture of the proud father. Laughingly he ruffled the little boy's hair. "Even when he says just a few words he can be heard—from far away. Ah yes, he is going to be an actor one day."

Kimberly lifted one brow. "Now where do you suppose he got that kind of talent?"

"I guess it was only natural." He bent down to give her a kiss on the cheek. "Forsooth, we might think of putting him in one of the plays. *A Midsummer Night's Dream,* perhaps."

She shook her head. "Not now, Christopher. He's much too shy."

"Shy?" Grinning at his son, he whispered, "I have little reason to attach that word to him."

"I know but—"

"Chris is still your baby, and you do not wish him to grow up too fast."

She loved him for understanding. "Maybe in a few years."

"A few years," he noted, smiling to himself as he thought about all those days he had stubbornly put settling down from his mind. If only he'd known what he'd been missing he'd have taken Kimberly Bowen to the altar much sooner. Being married to her was even better than he had dreamed it would be.

"Are you happy, Christopher?"

"Happier than I have ever been in my life." Just to show her that he meant it, Christopher placed his mouth upon hers, delighting in the pleasure her love always brought him. Love was the secret of life, the reason for being, the most precious thing that anyone could ever be given.